Sweet Little Thing

ABBI GLINES

#1 *NEW YORK TIMES* BESTSELLING AUTHOR

Sweet Little Thing

Prologue

IF ONLY MY backpack were larger it would be easier to hide the presents I got today. It was sweet of the boys to think of me. I especially loved the pink teddy bear with the "Be Mine" red heart in its hand. Its fur was so soft and pretty. I'd never been given anything like that before. The chocolate candies and heart-shaped necklace were also nice, but the bear was my favorite.

Tucking them all close to me to hide them while I rode the bus home was the hard part. I had to because I was afraid someone would take them. I'd already prepared myself to hand over the necklace and chocolates first if Harriet Boyd came after my things. She was six inches taller than me and tough like a boy. I was pretty sure the bus driver, Ms. V, was scared of Harriet too.

Getting home with the pink teddy bear Davey Eaton gave me was my goal. The other presents I could part with.

Davey was cute. He was also rich and popular. I imagined the bear cost a lot. It didn't look like the ones I'd seen at the pharmacy or grocery store all month. It was special—the kind of special I'd never gotten and would likely never get again. So, I was keeping the bear close.

Out of the three boys who gave me Valentine's Day gifts, I didn't like one any more than the other. All the boys were nice to me and seemed to like me. I knew that before they gave me gifts.

Momma told me not to worry about boyfriends in the third grade. But after getting the presents, I thought I might need to pick one. Maybe it would stop them from fighting over who got to sit by me at lunch.

I took a quick glance around me. I never made eye contact with Harriet if it was at all possible. Her voice was so loud, I knew she was only a few rows behind me. She was taunting someone about their hair.

My bus stop was next. I needed to make it to my stop, and then I'd be free. Safe from her bullying and possibly stealing my gifts.

Harriet hadn't bothered me too much this year. There was a girl who sat three rows back on the bus that had red hair and her teeth poked out a little too far in the front. Harriet was mean to her. I wished I was bigger. Or older. That way I could take up for the girl three rows back. But I was smaller than Harriet, and younger. Nothing I said would sway her. And today I had a teddy bear that needed to get home safely.

The bus slowed to a stop in front of my trailer park.

I made it.

I glanced back at the girl Harriet was harassing. I wanted to say something to help the other girl. But the bear in my hands kept me from doing anything. Not that anything I could have done would have helped anyway.

I quickly exited the bus, hurrying down the gravel road that was lined with oak trees and random empty beer cans. The grass was overgrown, and there were ant beds piled high on both sides of the road. I didn't study any of it long because I was in a hurry.

The blue single-wide trailer that I called home was faded from the sun. I'd imagine it was pretty at one time, but that had to have been years ago. Now it was old, and most of the siding was broken or missing. Momma said the trailer was all she could afford in rent. It had window units that cooled us in the summer, and we had a cranky heater that warmed us in the winter. The roof worked just fine. I figured we had it good.

When I stepped onto the overgrown grass in front of our trailer, the front door swung open.

"Beulah!" My sister's high-pitched voice carried across the yard when she shouted my name.

Heidi didn't go to school yet, even though we were only three minutes apart in age. Momma said she would be ready for school in a few years. I'd worried a lot that Heidi would never start, but Momma said there were special classes for her. I hadn't seen these special classes and hoped Momma was right.

"I have you a surprise," I told Heidi as I met her halfway when she ran out to hug me like she did every day. Heidi was my favorite person—even over our momma. She was happy no matter what. She loved you even when you were having a bad day and acted ugly. She was the perfect person and I wished everyone was like Heidi. I wondered why Momma said she was slow and she didn't fit in with everyone else.

She clapped her hands and squealed in delight. "What?" she asked.

I liked making her happy. I knew the moment I was given this bear today that Heidi would love it. I slipped my hand into the book bag and pulled out the bear.

Just like I had imagined, her eyes lit up as she grabbed it, hugging it tightly. Because of the look on her face I would tell Davey tomorrow that I would be his girlfriend—he'd made my sister smile.

"For me?" she asked her eyes wide.

I nodded. "Yes. For you. Happy Valentine's Day," I told her. Although I knew she didn't understand, like she didn't understand or care how I got the teddy bear.

She hugged it, tucking the teddy bear under her chin.

"I love you, Beulah," she said against the ears of the bear that was pressed to her mouth.

"I love you, Heidi," I told her.

Her smile was so big that I smiled too. It was a smile that only Heidi could give you. The one where no matter what was wrong with the world, you knew it was okay. I didn't have a memory that Heidi wasn't in. She was my twin. My sister. My other half. But she was different. She couldn't live life the way I did. She had to do it differently. All because she was a special angel God had sent to earth. I knew that was true. And I knew I'd always do anything to take care of her.

Chapter One

10 YEARS LATER

TODAY SHOULD BE special, but it was like any other day. Just another day that I existed, like all the others for the past six months. Keeping my head down and doing all that was asked of me was the one way I could make sure everything important to me was safe. Protected.

I woke up each day with a mission and hope that eventually my life would get better. That my current situation wasn't forever.

"Beulah, for God's sake, could you hurry with my coffee and get started on Jasper's room before he gets home? I haven't seen him in over eight months. His room needs to be perfect. Not that he'll stay long," Portia Van Allan called from the dining room.

Portia didn't eat food. At least, she didn't eat often. She drank coffee and she drank wine. Because of this, I wasn't expected to cook for her. The list of duties she had me do daily were enough to keep me busy from the time the sun came up to well after it went down.

"Yes ma'am," I replied as I finished making the French press coffee she preferred. It took time to brew the coffee unlike a regular coffee maker. The glass contraption also only made a cup with each press. It was one of the many things I hadn't ever heard of until I was forced to take the position as a maid in her home. When my mother gave me Portia's name and address on a piece of paper only a day before she passed away, I never asked who Portia was. I was so scared and in denial because of my mother's illness that it wasn't important at the time.

The day after my mother was buried, the landlord came to tell us we owed two months' rent on the trailer we lived in, and although he was very sorry for our loss, we had to pay or move out. I'd taken Heidi with me to Portia Van Allen's address that day, not knowing what to expect. Her home, where I now lived and worked, was not even close to what I had ever expected.

"I know he won't stay at the house long, but while he's here you'll make him breakfast. I'll ask him to leave you a list of what he eats. I can't remember because I never cooked for him. We had someone do that. His father liked French toast, I do remember that." Portia's words trailed off.

She looked up as I handed her cup of coffee to her, inspecting the coffee with great scrutiny.

"This seems darker than usual." She frowned although there were no frown lines on her face. I was sure Botox was the reason why. I wasn't sure how old she was, but she had a son in college.

"I made it the same way I make it every morning." Arguing with Portia was never a wise idea but sometimes I couldn't help myself. Like at this moment.

She started to open her mouth when noise from the front door stopped her. Loud voices and laughter rang out down the hall followed by the sound of clattering footsteps.

Confused, I glanced back at Portia.

She was sitting with her back straight, listening. "He's already here! Shit!"

I assumed "he" was her son since no one ever walked into this house without a key. They couldn't even get past the privacy gate without a code.

She jumped up and looked frantic. "He has company. I need to get dressed." She hurried for the back stairs that lead to the master bedroom. "Feed them. Take care of them," were her last words before she disappeared around the corner. Her black French-press coffee was forgotten on the table.

I wasn't ready to face an unknown Van Allen. The one I knew wasn't exactly a pleasant person. I had hoped I wouldn't have to see her son that much while he was home. Only when I served his breakfast maybe. But this . . . this was not what I had planned on.

I walked down the small hallway that separated the kitchen from the dining room and ducked into the kitchen to hide until her son and whoever was with him went upstairs. Maybe he would look for Portia. God knew he wouldn't look in the kitchen.

As I entered the kitchen from the dining room entrance, the opposite entrance swung open.

"My mother doesn't eat, but she knew I was coming so there should be something. Help yourselves, but if there is some of Ms. Charlotte's peanut butter pie in here it's mine." He was addressing the group walking with him into the kitchen.

I had seen family photos around the house. I knew Jasper Van Allen was handsome. However, seeing him in person—his blonde hair messy as if he had just run his hand through it, and the way his clothes fit his tall, lean but muscular build—was a sight to see.

He turned from the people who were following him, saw me and paused. His gaze slowly took me in and I felt nervous. I didn't like to be studied. And I had no idea what to say to him. I hadn't made eye contact yet, but there were three guys behind him. I could see their bodies but I wasn't looking at them.

"You're not Ms. Charlotte," were the words he spoke that finally broke the sudden and awkward silence.

No, I wasn't. I was her replacement. She'd retired and moved to Florida with her granddaughter.

I was about to tell him that when he let out a short, unamused laugh. "Guess I won't be getting that peanut butter pie."

"If you'd like breakfast, I could make you something," I said, hoping he would take the hint that I didn't want to cook for them and would leave.

"Who the hell are you?" he asked with disgust. "Portia isn't one to hire hot young girls that don't know how to do shit."

I had thought he was attractive. For a moment. That moment was now gone.

"Beulah Edwards. I took Ms. Charlotte's place when she retired." I wanted to say more—to inform his elitist cocky ass I was as good as Ms. Charlotte. But I wasn't sure that was a true statement, so I just held my tongue.

"Seriously? Jesus, is my mother hitting the fucking bourbon again?"

The boys behind him laughed like what he'd said was hilarious. I hadn't looked at the others yet. Straightening up and holding my shoulders back, I turned with my now angry glare to look at the rest of them. They were the same. Tall, athletic, wealthy and their arrogance hung on them like a gilded chain. They knew nothing of work or hunger. They knew no fear. They knew nothing but easy living. I didn't normally hate anyone for those reasons, but this bunch was making me think being elite was a disease.

I noticed one of them wasn't laughing. He looked like them and dressed like them. He was better looking than was fair like them. But he was different. Instead of a wearing a look of amusement, he appeared bored. As if he was honoring everyone else with his presence was a waste of his time. In a way, his expression was more demeaning than the laughter.

"Just merlot. Nightly. Three to four glasses depending on her mood." I wanted to appear as bored as the dark-haired boy. As unaffected and as if this conversation was a waste of my time. Because it was.

Jasper Van Allen smirked then. "Well, Beulah, can you make omelets? Bacon? Or is there any of that in this house?"

Portia had sent me to the grocery store yesterday with an extensive list of items for the kitchen. "Yes, to both. And yes, we have those things."

"Portia must have had food delivered then," he said turning to look back at the guys with him. "We can take our shit to the pool house."

The pool house was not where Portia was expecting Jasper to stay. Nor was she expecting him to arrive with guests. I didn't expect either of those things would make her very happy. She'd be popping one or more of the little white pills she ate like candy once she found out about Jasper's plans.

"The pool house hasn't been prepared. Your mother expected you to stay in your room." Not that his room was prepared either since he had arrived early.

Jasper paused from his retreat and turned back to look at me.

I didn't like the smirk on his face, or the gleam of amusement with a touch of pity in his eyes. "Portia doesn't own this house, so I'd say that it doesn't matter what she expects."

He didn't enlighten me any further. He just turned and left the room. The others followed. I stood there wondering what exactly he had meant by that because Heidi's safety was resting on Portia's shoulders.

Chapter Two

WHILE MAKING THE omelets and bacon, I tried to figure out what he meant when he said that Portia didn't own the house. Who else would own it? Was she in financial trouble? That was my main concern because I needed her. Heidi and I needed her.

"How many are here?" Portia asked as she swept into the kitchen dressed as if she were about to do a fashion shoot for a magazine.

"Three, plus Jasper," I told her as I glanced up from the last omelet in the pan.

"The little shit. He could have told me he was bringing friends home. I wasn't prepared to entertain anyone." She paced back and forth a few moments and then took a drink from the glass in her hand. The glass was from the bar—a whiskey glass with amber liquid in it. I didn't see what the big deal was, but I had learned Portia was a dramatic woman. "Are they all out at the pool house?"

she asked as she stared at the door that led in that direction.

"Yes."

She sighed. "Well, there is that. They can drink and throw their parties out there. I thought his days of bringing home his fraternity brothers were over. That it was time he assumed his responsibilities. But no. He brings home," she waved her drink in the direction of the pool house, "them."

There were several questions that flew through my mind. Like why was it bad Jasper brought his friends home? Didn't she expect Jasper to stay for a short visit and leave anyway? What responsibilities did Jasper need to assume?

I held my tongue and didn't ask any questions. Their issues were not my business and she'd let me know that if I asked.

AS I ADDED fresh berries to the plates with their omelets, the guys walked back into the house. The sound of their voices carried our way from the dining room.

I would serve them, find out what they wanted to drink, and then I'd go about the rest of my day cleaning and anything else Portia asked of me. Hopefully, I didn't have to clean the pool house.

"Go feed them," she said with a sour look as she pointed in the direction of the four loud guys. "While they're eating, head outside and prepare the pool house. When you are done with that, buy them food and stock the bar out there as well. The less they have to come inside the house the better." With that she spun on her heel and sashayed out of the kitchen but not before putting her drink down. Guess she didn't want Jasper to see her drinking before noon.

I took the first two plates and followed behind Portia to the dining room.

"Hello, Jasper. I'm sorry I wasn't prepared for your early arrival," Portia said as if she were thrilled to see him. "Sterling, Tate, Winston. I'm so glad you boys could come for a visit. I trust you're all doing well."

Jasper, Sterling, Tate, and Winston? Did these people not have any Henry, Chad, Jack, or Tim's? I'd never heard names like theirs. However, my senior class had three Chad's, three Hanks, three David's, and two Jacks.

Then again, my name was Beulah, so who was I to talk. My sister got the better name. Which fit because out of the two of us she was the best. Heidi was perfect. If the world could love like her, find joy the way she did, and smile her smile, we'd all be so much happier.

"Yes, ma'am," Jasper's ginger-haired friend said. I wasn't sure what his name was. "Mother said the two of you won your tennis match last week. Congratulations on that."

Portia played tennis daily. It was one of many activities she did with her friends. She beamed at his recognition. I noticed Jasper rolling his eyes. Then his eyes locked with mine and he winked. I jerked my gaze away, and sat the food down in front of the ginger and the dark-haired elitist guy, who was still quiet and seemed to be looking down his nose at everyone. As if no one were on his level, or could ever hope to be.

"Thank you, Tate. We deserved it of course. Camille and I have worked so hard."

I left the room for the other two plates of food. The small talk continued as Portia went on and on about her tennis game. When I returned with the last of the food, Portia had taken a seat at the end of the table opposite Jasper.

"I'll need a fresh cup of coffee," she informed me.

"About that. What happened to Ms. Charlotte? And who is she?" I didn't look his way although my entire body went taut. He wasn't pleased I was here. I'd done everything he'd asked of me so far but that didn't seem to matter.

"Charlotte retired. She moved to be near her grandchildren. She was getting up there in age, Jasper. I needed more help than she was able to provide."

"You didn't think to ask me before replacing her?" The tone of his voice wasn't what I'd expect from a son talking to his to a mother. It was more of a threat. Or correction. As if he were the boss and she was an employee.

"Don't be so damn rude to your mom," Tate said, dressing Jasper down. I had to agree. Portia wasn't the nicest woman I knew, but she'd taken Heidi and me in without a question or any explanation. She just did it. I owed her so much for that.

Jasper, however, ignored the comment and continued to glare in his mother's direction. Then he turned his attention to me. "We'll need drinks if we don't want to choke on our food."

I felt my face heat from the nasty tone in his voice. "I'm sorry. I was waiting on your conversation to end before I interrupted to ask what I could get you."

"It's okay, love. He's just testy because his girlfriend Maisie ended things with him while she's off gallivanting in Europe for the summer. He'll recover his broken heart soon enough and be as charming as ever. And I'm Sterling by the way." Sterling had a nice smile that displayed perfect white teeth. His brown hair had golden sun streaks in it. Like the others, he looked like he belonged to this set. But he was nice.

"Maisie broke things off? Do her parents know?" Portia

sounded horrified.

"She's a twenty-one-year old woman, Mother. I don't think it matters if her parents know or not. Now let's drop the subject."

"I'll take a coffee. Black," Sterling told me with a kind smile.

"Same," Tate said from across the table.

"Milk," Jasper added, turning his gaze my way, a small apologetic smile touched his lips. He was odd. His attitude went from angry to nice so easily.

I turned to look at the quiet guy. The one who had to be named Winston since the other names had been taken. He made me nervous. His boredom made it feel as if he judged everything quietly. "Water," he said without making eye contact with me. His nonchalance made me feel as if I didn't exist. I was beneath him. He was making sure that message was delivered loud and clear.

I hurried from the room with their drink orders. When I started waiting tables at Pizza Pit four years ago, I'd been thrilled to get that job. Now I was thankful I had the experience. Because never once in those years of daydreaming had I thought I'd be waiting on people like this. I was supposed to be in college getting my nursing degree. And my mother was supposed to live a long time. She was supposed to be there to watch me grow up and make my way in the world. And to always be there for Heidi. Mom and Heidi were supposed to be my home. I'd never imagined this would be our future.

My dream of someday working in the pediatric ward of a hospital would never come true now. I had more to worry about than lost dreams. When mother died, she left Heidi to me. And I wouldn't let anything happen to take that smile off Heidi's face. A face that should have looked like mine. Although our eyes were the same color, not much else was the same. Heidi was different, but beautifully so.

I didn't use the French press for the coffees because they didn't ask. I used the fancy machine that normally sat on the kitchen counter collecting dust to make them each a cup of coffee while I made Portia's the way she always insisted. I took one of the frozen mugs from the freezer that Portia had told me were for Jasper's milk two days ago when she asked me to freeze them. I thought the icy mugs sounded nice. Ice cold milk. I almost used one for the water that Mr. I'm-Too-Good-For-Others had asked for, but decided against it. He didn't deserve any special treatment.

Wheeling a cart from the pantry, I used it as a drink tray, placing each of their drinks on it. I was kicking myself because I should have used this contraption for their meals. I could have taken all four plates at one time, but I hadn't thought of the cart until I went into the pantry to get the coffee cups and saw it there.

Walking back into the dining room I heard Portia say. "All summer? But why? You normally travel in the summer."

My stomach dropped. Surely she didn't mean Jasper was planning to stay here all summer. A few days of this I could take, but an entire summer?

I briefly closed my eyes and pictured Heidi's sweet smile. I could do this. I could do anything.

Chapter Three

I WAS GIVEN one day off every week to visit Heidi. The place that Portia paid for her to stay had family day on Sunday, and I visited rain or shine. We ate picnics I had prepared outside under the oak trees at the home. We played kickball, and I pushed Heidi on one of the many swings in the large backyard there.

The facility was always full of families and visitors. Heidi had one friend, however, that didn't ever have family visit. She also had Down syndrome. Her name was May.

It bothered Heidi when May was left alone, so we made her a part of our family. I gave her the same special cookie treats I gave Heidi, and she played with us every Sunday. It was what I looked forward to every week. It was all I looked forward to.

But today, I wouldn't be able to see my sister. Today, I would miss my visit. When I called Heidi to explain, she was sad. She didn't say so, but her voice was quieter. It hurt my heart so much. I hated this. I also hated the people outside at the pool keeping me from visiting my sister. They were all spoiled, wealthy, rude, and full of themselves. All of them.

To add to the mayhem, the four boys had multiplied. As the music had gotten louder, the pool area and pool house got busier. The back of the house was alive and overrun with the guests Jasper had over.

I had been running in and out of the main house, keeping ice buckets filled with fresh ice, making sure beer was available, and that the bar was stocked with supplies for mixed drinks. When some blonde who looked like she could use a cheeseburger asked me to fetch her a glass of sparkling water and make sure the bubbles were tiny, I almost shoved her into the pool.

How was one supposed to make bubbles tiny? Did I blow on it a specific way? Or possibly spit in it? Because I liked the idea of spitting in it.

Hurrying back inside, I almost ran into Portia who once again had a glass of whiskey in her hand. It was just after two o'clock in the afternoon. I wasn't judging, but I wondered if this visit was going to drive her to alcoholism.

"You can go tomorrow. Not all day of course. But for a few hours," Portia said to me apologetically.

I paused. Then I looked at her and nodded my understanding. "Thank you." She knew I was upset and she knew why. Another reason I felt Portia wasn't all bad.

She grimaced. "Don't. I'm just saying you can go for a few hours. They'll call if you don't visit. I would rather not deal with the drama." With a flounce of her skirt, she walked away. The way her blonde hair floated as she moved reminded me of my mother. I missed my mother. She was nothing like Portia, but that one movement made me remember a happier time. Even if it was Portia that reminded me.

The ache in my chest eased knowing I would see Heidi tomorrow. I could take cupcakes—she loved them. That wouldn't make up for today, but at least it would make her happy and she'd feel special and loved. I never wanted her to feel forgotten. Momma had never made her feel any different than other kids. I knew the home she lived in made her feel different now. But there was no other choice. Portia didn't want her at her house.

"Do you know the difference in sparkling waters?" a deep voice asked me. Startled, I turned to see Winston standing there shirtless. He was wearing a pair of shorts that hung on his hips showing off a muscular build that was hard not to stare at. But I disliked him enough to ignore it.

"Why?" I asked him as I walked away.

He didn't respond and I kept walking. He wasn't my boss. He was the rude friend. I didn't feel the need to listen to him make fun of my lack of sparkling water knowledge.

I could feel him following behind me. I wished he wouldn't, but other than turning to tell him to go the hell away I was stuck with him. And Jasper didn't care for me. At least, that was my guess. He wanted Ms. Charlotte and I wasn't her. Making his friends angry wouldn't help me keep this job. I needed to make this guy like me or at least approve of me.

Opening the fridge that contained ridiculous amounts of different waters—sparkling, mineral, and spring—I reached for the Perrier because differentiating bubble size made no sense.

"La Croix, not the Perrier," Winston said from where he was watching behind me. "Smaller bubbles. It's a fresher taste. Not that I think Isla knows the difference."

I wanted to ignore him, but I didn't want to deal with this

Isla if I got her the wrong water, so I put the Perrier back and grabbed the La Croix. "Thanks," I said begrudgingly, and then turned to head back outside.

"You'll need a glass of ice to give her with that."

He was right. I should have thought of that, but his presence was annoying me so it escaped me. Without looking at him, I went back into the kitchen and got the glass and ice while he stood there. Was he waiting to see if there was something else he could correct for me?

Before I exited the kitchen again, he spoke up. "He'll start to flirt with you. He won't mean it. It's Jasper. But when you flirt back, you'll be gone. You're the help."

I wanted to say a lot of things at that moment. I wanted to throw the glass of ice I was holding in his face. I wanted to tell him to kiss my ass. I wanted to tell him I didn't flirt with guys like them. But I bit my tongue because tomorrow I had plans. I had someone in my life and that was more important than all the harsh words I could say to him.

I started to walk away again. I hoped to scuttle off without hearing his deep southern drawl speaking more demeaning words that were delivered with what would be an attractive sound.

"I didn't mean to offend you. But girls like you get that look in your eyes. You see a fairy tale. One this life doesn't have for you. I thought I'd stop it before you made a mistake."

It seemed each time he opened his mouth his words were more offensive. But he claims he doesn't mean to offend me? Seriously?

Walking away was what I should have done. But it wasn't what I chose to do.

"You don't know me." I stopped myself from saying any

more. He didn't know me nor did he deserve to. I held back the other words that lingered, threatening to spill out and tell him exactly what I thought of him.

He let me go when I walked away without spouting additional rude, offensive, meaningless garbage from his overly attractive mouth.

Outside, the music was almost deafening and I had no idea how anyone was capable of hearing the person next to them talk. Two girls had decided to go topless and were sitting on the edge of the pool splashing water with a new guy that had arrived, Tate. I scanned the crowd to find Isla had moved from her previous spot and was now wrapped around Jasper. She was still in the tiny bikini she was wearing, but I figured she'd drop her top soon. Especially if Jasper's attention stayed on the topless blonde flirting with Tate.

"Your sparkling water," I said not wanting Jasper to see me and think I was there to ask him anything.

"Oh," she said turning to take the water from me. She didn't look thrilled about having to stop touching Jasper. I felt his gaze on me but didn't make eye contact.

"Thank you, Beulah," he said, surprising me.

I did glance up at him then and gave him a small nod before turning to walk away. He wasn't flirting—he was only being nice. But Winston's demeaning words still roamed through my head. I'd be careful in case there was any truth to them. I didn't want to be accused of flirting. That was the last thing I wanted or needed.

"We need more ice for the beer," a male voice called out. I hurried to do that. Then I went to make some guy a grilled cheese sandwich with chips. When I delivered that, more of the guys began placing similar orders. The day went on and on. A caterer showed up at four to handle dinner. I helped the caterers serve dinner and hoped the party would end soon.

Very few girls were wearing tops. Some were even missing bottoms.

Three guys were also going bare. I'd never seen so many naked bodies in my life.

"I want to see that one topless," a drunk guy yelled out as I placed another tray of fancy shrimp on crackers near the cabana. I turned to see him pointing at me.

"She's the help dumbass," a girl told him.

"I want to know where the fuck Jasper hired help that looks like that. I'll take five or ten."

"You're cut off Auden," Jasper's voice came from my left. Much closer than I'd expected. He was lounging with Isla at his side and like I guessed earlier she was topless. They both had drinks and his hand was now inside her bikini, splayed across her bottom.

"Don't tell me you don't want to see her naked," he said laughing.

"That'll be all for tonight, Beulah. You can head to your room." Jasper's tone sounded as if he were talking to a child. However, I nodded and mustered my self respect as I walked back into the house with my shoulders straight and my head held high.

I'd cry a later, but I'd do it in the shower when I washed off the day and I could be alone.

Chapter Four

THE NOISE FROM the partying group was muffled inside the house. The further I walked away and the closer I got to the back stairs, their chaos was quieter.

My room was downstairs next to the laundry room, wine cellar, and storage. The bed that I slept on was full-sized and was in the corner of the same room as the washer and dryer. Their location made it convenient to doing laundry at night. Before Jasper and his friends came there had been very little laundry. Now the piles would be endless, towels mostly I suspected.

I had opened the door that led to my room, but the clicking of heels stopped me from going any further. Portia appeared from around the corner. Another glass of the amber liquid she had been drinking all day was in her hand. She looked annoyed and concerned at the same time.

"I saw Jasper talking to you not once, but several times. And he was looking at you. Make yourself less attractive. He'll get rid of you and I won't be able to do anything about it. If you want this job and to take care of your sister, then don't draw his attention." The last word came out in an angry hiss, then she turned and walked away quickly. Her clicking heels on the marble floor were slowly drowned out by the sound of the party.

I walked down the stairs slowly. Partly because I was tired, partly because I was frustrated, and partly because I was scared. Since coming here I'd been worried that what I had could end. That Portia would get mad at me stope everything. Just as I began to trust that I was safe, Jasper showed up and I'm told by two people that he would get rid of me.

Why did Jasper get to make that decision? Who was he that he could tell his mother what to do? And how did she expect me to make myself less attractive?

I had no mirror down here, but I could look down and see the knee length khaki shorts and white polo shirt that Portia had given me for my job. Nothing about this outfit was attractive. I reached up, touching my hair that was pulled back tightly in a ponytail. Some of the girls by the pool looked like a stylist had done their messy updos. The girls weren't really clothed anymore, but when they were, their bikinis had been sexy and expensive. I couldn't possibly stand out in a crowd like that. They saw me and knew I was the help. There wasn't any way I could make myself less attractive.

Sighing, I sank down on the edge of the bed and kicked off my tennis shoes. My feet hurt every night because the shoes Portia had given me were a size six and I wore an eight. After running around all day and not even getting a break for lunch, my toes were so cramped that the pain from setting them free took my breath away.

My stomach rumbled and I looked toward the stairs knowing there was no way I could get food and go unnoticed. My feet ached more than my stomach did. I'd make sure to eat breakfast before I had to start my day tomorrow.

It was almost midnight. I'd be up again in six hours. The shower was beside the washing machine. It was inside a clawfoot tub that had a wraparound curtain. Standing up, I winced and hobbled over on my sore feet to turn the warm water on. A good cry would make me feel better, and the hot water would feel wonderful on my feet.

When I finally laid down in bed, sleep came fast. Faster than normal.

Luckily, I wasn't so exhausted that I slept past six, when I was supposed to be up. My stomach was growling when I opened my eyes and I figured that was what had woken me. With a good long stretch, I wiggled my feet. They were still sore but better after rest. The idea of putting the too small shoes back on made me grimace. It was early and no one would be awake until at least nine. I could head upstairs in my socks. My breakfast would be so much more enjoyable if my feet weren't cramped up.

I dressed quickly, pulled my hair back in a ponytail, brushed my teeth and headed for the stairs. This was my favorite time of day. It was the only time I had to myself that I could enjoy. Now that Jasper and his friends were here for the summer I'd look forward to my early mornings even more. Especially if yesterday was any indication of how he planned on spending his summer.

Portia had bragged about Jasper to her friends that visited, and acted like him being home was a wonderful thing. Then he'd arrived and it all changed. She completely changed. The woman who had been distant and unfeeling seemed scared of her son.

That made no sense to me. I was missing something and I wanted to know what.

Before I walked into the kitchen, I heard a cabinet close. Who the heck was in there this early? Portia didn't stir until after ten o'clock on most days. I doubted she'd ever seen six in the morning. Ever. In her life.

I peeked around the corner to find a girl with messy dark brown hair. A large guys T-shirt was the only thing covering her body. She was on her tiptoes looking in the cabinets. I assumed she was one of Jasper's guests from last night. Which meant I had to help her. She was ruining my quiet morning.

"Can I get you something?" I asked as I walked all the way into the kitchen.

She dropped to the flats of her feet and spun around to look at me. "Oh. It's you. Yeah, I need some coffee and food. I've got work in an hour. Do you know how to call a cab around here?"

Work? She worked? "Uh, I don't know about a cab but you could Google it on your phone. I'm sure you could use an app for a car service too. Those come here."

She sighed. "Yeah, that'd be great if I had a phone with an app, and those car services require bank cards attached to them, and I don't have one of those either. I have ten bucks. And that ten bucks has to get me to my apartment so I can get dressed."

This girl didn't sound like one of Jasper's friends. At least, not one of the Ivy league, trust fund types I'd met so far. It was interesting that she was here.

Unable to help myself I asked, "Where do you work?"

She walked over to the fridge. "I nanny for Auden Elswood's younger siblings. His father's second wife is twenty-seven and they have two-year-old twin terrors. A boy and girl. That's how I know this crowd since you're obviously trying to figure me out. Now could you point me to food?"

"Oh, yeah. I was going to make myself some eggs and bacon. You want some?"

She shook her head. "Don't have time. A muffin maybe? And a cup of coffee to go?"

I walked over to the pantry and found the bakery muffins that Portia sometimes nibbled on with her coffee in the morning. Stepping out, I handed it to her and went over to make the coffee.

"Thank you. I'm so damn hungry."

"You're welcome," I replied.

"I'm Shay by the way. I saw you working last night. Thought it looked about as sucky as my job. But then you get to see Jasper every day, so that's a perk. I hear he's an amazing fuck."

Opening the cabinet where there were less expensive coffee cups, I reached in and took one down. There were no disposable cups here but this one wouldn't be missed. I didn't really want to discuss Jasper or his sex life. I preferred to ignore that comment.

"Do you have a name?"

I was being rude and she was the friendliest person I'd met here yet. "Beulah."

Shay scrunched her nose. "Weird name."

I nodded. Because I agreed. I'd never much cared for my name. But now my mother was gone and I didn't complain anymore. It was something no one could take away from me.

"That was rude. Sorry. I just say stuff. I have no filter," Shay said quietly.

"No, it's okay. It is an odd name. My mother gave it to me, and now that she's gone I cherish it."

Shay winced. "Damn, I really am sorry. I should work on that.

I didn't know my mom. Or my dad. G-maw raised me—that was what we called the older lady in the foster home where I lived for twelve years. She passed away just before I turned eighteen. Cancer got her. She smoked every day."

"Oh, I'm sorry to hear that."

Shay grinned. "About my suck life or G-maw passing?"

"Both," I replied honestly.

"Me too. But don't sound or look like your life is peaches either. We're making it fine enough though. Could be worse. Always could be worse. Anyway, I gotta go. I'll walk until I figure out the cab thing. Someone may give me a ride. Nice talking to you and thanks for the coffee and muffin."

THEN SHE HEADED for the door. In a T-shirt. Only a T-shirt.

Chapter Five

JASPER'S GUESTS DIDN'T come inside for breakfast. People began to wake outside on lounge chairs, and stumbled out of the pool house slowly. Before lunch, the place had cleared out. Portia had drunk two cups of coffee and watched the exodus from the living room with a frown.

She ate a bowl of fruit, then finally gave me the go ahead to leave. I had three hours to see Heidi.

She didn't want to explain to Jasper where I had gone if he came inside asking for food, or washed clothing or decided on having another party. My mother's 1998 Honda Civic still ran with almost two hundred thousand miles on it. I kept it parked in the spot that Ms. Charlotte had kept her car. If I hadn't needed the little bit of gas I had left to see Heidi today I would have offered to give Shay a ride. But my fuel was precious. I was given just enough a month in gas money from Portia to drive back and forth once a week to Among the Spanish Moss, the special needs home where Heidi lived now.

My time to see her was limited today, so I didn't make my stops to say hello to the other residents I'd come to know. I did stop by the nurse's desk to drop cupcakes off for all of them. I had made them before Jasper had gotten home and had stashed them away. I normally made cookies every week and brought them. It wasn't much but I wanted to bring them something as a thank you for being so good to Heidi. They seemed to love their jobs and were good with the residents.

"Beulah, I'm so happy to see you. There is a girl that woke up extra early and has been making her rounds telling everyone you were coming today. She's excited."

Heidi was a socializer. She liked to visit all her friends and talk to the nurses. Staying in her room or the activity room wasn't enough for her. She didn't sit and watch television much. Although she did enjoy the craft sessions they set up for them every day. She liked anything involving glitter. The shinier she could make something the better. It couldn't sparkle enough for her.

"Where is she now?" I asked, anxious to see her.

"Oh, she's in her room. Wearing her purple dress with the glitter flowers on it that she loves so much. She wouldn't wear it yesterday because she said you weren't coming so she was too sad to wear it. But don't worry. She ended up going outside and playing after her sulk was over."

I'd make up for that the best I could. I had three cupcakes left for Heidi, May, and me. We would walk out to the lawn and watch the ducks at the pond while we ate our cupcakes and they told me all about their week.

Before I reached Heidi's door it swung open, and out bounced Heidi.

"Is Beulah—" she started to ask loudly to anyone that heard her in the hallway then paused when she saw me. Her face lit up and the smile I loved spread brightly. "Beulah!" she cried gleefully, and then ran to me.

I sat the bag that held the cupcakes on the ground beside me just in time to catch her as she threw her arms around me. In all my life, no one had ever been as excited to see me as Heidi. She was always excited to see me.

"Hey, beautiful! I missed you yesterday," I told her hugging her back just as tightly.

"I missed you," she said still clinging to me. "We played ball and I had a cookie. Chocolate chip."

"Your favorite kind! That's wonderful. Did May have one too?" I asked.

"Yes, she ate three but don't tell. She wasn't s'posed to." Heidi was whispering loudly.

I knew the nurses wouldn't care about the three cookies, but I went along with her serious expression. "Okay. I won't say a word. Our secret."

She nodded. "Locked it up an throw away the key," she said making the motion like she was locking up her lips.

"Done," I assured her. "I have a treat. Where's May? I brought her a treat too."

At the word treat, Heidi beamed again. All seriousness gone. "A treat! What kind?"

"The best kind."

"Oh boy," she said clapping. Then called toward the nurse's station. "Beulah brought me a treat!"

They all smiled and nodded.

She grabbed my hand and tugged, leading me toward the

activity room. "May is making paper dolls. I was waiting on you," Heidi explained plainly as we walked into the large room full of round tables filled with crafts.

The staff would have crafts set up for another hour, then it would change to board games for two hours, then coloring sheets, and then they would have instruments to play at the end of the day. Soothing classical music filled the room now, and residents talked and worked on their projects. May was sitting at a round red table studying the paper doll in her hands with intensity.

"I see her," Heidi exclaimed like that was the best news of the day and hurried to May calling her name.

May looked up and saw me. Her smile was as bright as my sister's. Heidi got to her and whispered in her ear. She knew better than to announce to the room that I had treats for them. Everyone would want one too. I wished I could afford to bring them all treats. One day, I'd get my degree and I'd have a career, and Heidi would move back in with me. We'd continue to visit and bring everyone treats.

May dropped her paper doll and they both came running back in my direction. "I told her," Heidi said. "Let's go see the ducks."

I let them lead the way and May gave me a shy smile and hug. She was quieter than Heidi. I knew her life had been more different than my sister's. She wasn't comfortable receiving love the way Heidi was. She was nervous. I tried to show her with every visit she could trust me. She was learning that I would accept her hug and give her one back.

The sun was beautiful and warm today. We found a nice shady spot, the girls got comfortable and then I handed them each a cupcake before taking mine and joining them. They both giggled with delight at the sight of the cupcakes.

I'd used ingredients from Portia's pantry to make them. Ms. Charlotte had left a lot of baking supplies behind. Portia never requested baked goods, so I used them to make things to bring to Heidi, May and the nurses. I hoped by the time the supplies ran out, I would have enough money to afford to restock.

They loved the cookies, and occasional cupcakes. One week, I'd made Rice Krispy treats. Then once I'd made brownies, but we were out of chocolate now. So I was making sugar cookies with sprinkles most of the time.

"This is the best cupcake I evah had," May told me licking her lips.

"Beulah is the best cooker," Heidi bragged. "Momma taught her and me to cook a lot. I can cook too."

May's eyes went wide with amazement even though Heidi had told her this story many times. And it was true. Momma had always let us help her with dinner. When there was extra money she'd make us sweets. I'd learned more from her than just baking and cooking skills. I'd learned how to love. Mom was the best teacher.

Chapter Six

" **I** THOUGHT WHEN you said you were ready to take over
your position at the corporation that you'd go to Boston,
Chicago, or even New York for the summer. I didn't expect you
to come here and bring all these people. You can't expect them to
take you seriously at Van Allan Industries if you're having topless
parties every day. They aren't just going to respect you because
your father named you CEO at his death."

I paused. Portia was talking, and although I hadn't walked
into the back yard yet, I knew it was Jasper she was talking to. I
didn't realize Van Allan Industries was now his. He was . . . not
ready for that. From the little bit I'd experienced from him, I
couldn't imagine the tall glass building in Manhattan known
as Van Allen Industries was now the responsibility of a spoiled,
partying, twenty-one-year-old.

"Don't recall asking you what you thought, Mother. Neither
did my father. But then you were so busy fucking the tennis pro

at the club you weren't paying attention to the will and Dad's last-minute changes. So, while you waste your breath telling me what I can and can't do, remember this is mine. All of it. Dad didn't care what happened to his unfaithful wife at his death. He had time to change his mind. But he didn't."

I backed away from the room. This was not my business. Wow! Their conversation was shocking though. It was not a subject I expected to hear them discuss. Jasper was cold. Angry and cold toward his mother. If she'd been having an affair, I understood his hurt. Especially since his father had died of a heart attack. But the complete emotionally detachment in his voice was shocking. He seemed so easygoing and carefree. Looks were deceiving. My mother had always told me that.

"I'm not going to defend myself to you. I am sorry for what I did but there were things in our marriage you knew nothing about. You're my son. I want you to succeed. That is all this is about. It's all I'm trying to say."

He laughed and it was a hard laugh. It wasn't real. I couldn't see his face, but the sound made me shiver. "You worry about your tea parties, tennis matches, and shopping trips. I'll handle everything else. Don't give me advice. You're not anyone I'd take it from."

There was silence, and then footsteps.

"Jasper, please," Portia called out, but a door slammed in the distance and I knew he had walked outside to the pool house.

I stood where I was to stay hidden and didn't move until I heard Portia walk away and enter the house. I waited five minutes before walking to the entrance I always used in the back yard near the kitchen. I didn't know what this family was like before Alfred Van Allan suffered a massive heart attack and died two days later, but I knew they were completely dysfunctional now. I felt sorry for Portia, although she didn't sound like she had made wise decisions. I also felt sorry for Jasper because he had obviously been raised to be the man he was. They'd created him.

I had been raised by a woman who luckily put her kids first, above all else. Even before having a social life. I never once saw her date.

"I'd forget all you heard. Wasn't your business," the deep drawl I now recognized as Winston's said from behind me. I was beginning to think he stalked me to catch me off guard and put me in my place. In his stuck-up, conceited world I was the minion he could look down on.

"I'm aware of that. It wasn't on purpose. I just got home," I snapped at him.

He gave a small shrug of his left shoulder, sat down on a lounger, then laid back and put his hands behind his head. "But you listened. You could have walked away."

He was right. I could have. I started to argue that they were blocking my entrance, but it sounded lame even to me.

Instead, I walked away from Winston. I didn't have to explain myself to him. I wasn't going to try.

"He won't keep you. She hired you, which makes him detest you. No matter how appealing you might be."

That was a fear I was trying not to focus on, but after hearing what I'd just—as he'd pointed out I eavesdropped on—Winston may be right. If he fired me, Heidi and I would be on the streets. How would I keep her fed? I couldn't afford the home where she lived, or leave her to work a job. Not alone. She couldn't be left alone. Especially not on the streets.

My head began to pound. I hurried inside to get away from

Winston and his threats. I couldn't lose this job. This job was all I had right now. Working here was keeping Heidi in a safe home. If my mother was friends with Portia, or Portia owed her something, I had no idea what that connection was, but I knew Jasper wouldn't care. He hated his mother, that much was obvious. He wouldn't care about helping Heidi or me.

"You're late," Portia said as I walked into the house. I was actually early but their talk outside had stalled me. I couldn't tell her I had overheard them though.

"I'm sorry. Traffic was bad."

She glared at me. "I did you a favor letting you go today. The least you could do was return on time. I don't need this from you. You're the help. The help. Do your damn job and stop acting so damn entitled." She slammed her glass down on the table causing the liquid to slosh over and drip down onto the floor. "Clean that up. Then get to your duties."

I nodded. "Yes ma'am."

She stalked from the room and I hurried to clean up her mess. I understood she was hurting over what her son had said to her. The bitterness and anger that often spewed from her came from that hurt. She'd had an unhappy life. She'd slept with another man. After her husband died, she was left to the mercy of her son. For a woman like Portia who lives in luxury, I imagine the threat of having her lifestyle taken away was tough. It didn't make her treatment of me all right, of course. But I understood it.

"She's a bitch, isn't she?" That was Jasper's voice. "You don't have to answer that. I know what you're thinking. Can't figure out why you're here working for her when you could work so many other places. That face—it could get you in many doors."

I finished wiping up her spilled drink from the floor and stood up to face him. "I hope I never have to use my face to get a job. And this job is just fine. It covers my needs and my feelings aren't hurt easily." I hoped that was the right thing to say.

He studied me. That made me nervous as I waited for him to respond. It seemed much longer than the seconds it took. "You want this job then?"

"Yes."

He shrugged and sighed. "Fine. She's hard to deal with. If you can handle her, then you'll do. You handled last night like a fucking champ. I was impressed."

Portia never complimented me. I wasn't sure if a thank you was appropriate or not. "I was doing my job."

Jasper chuckled. "Yeah. I guess you were," was his response, then he walked out the door heading toward the pool house. I watched as he said something to Winston, who laughed, and I stopped to watch that. Winston laugh. All I had ever seen was his serious face. And the disinterested way he looked down on all around those him. I hadn't seen him smile. His face that was stunning with a scowl became almost angelic with a smile.

Shaking my head, I stopped admiring him and went to the kitchen. I had my list in there for the things I needed to do today. Staring at Winston wasn't one of them.

Chapter Seven

BY THE NEXT morning, no one remained at the pool house but Jasper. The others had left last night. I'd seen their expensive cars drive away. I wasn't sure if they would return or if Jasper would be moving into his bedroom. I did know that today I had to clean the pool house. He'd told me not to worry about it yesterday but to come back after nine in the morning and give it a heavy cleaning. He would also leave a grocery list for me.

I watched him walk out at eight-thirty this morning, dressed in a suit with his messy blond hair brushed, and I had to admit he was stunning. He didn't look like a CEO. He looked like a GQ magazine cover model. But he was obviously going to work somewhere. I wasn't sure if they had offices in Savannah. Apparently, Van Allen Industries had something here.

I heard the sound of heels clicking on the marble floor and knew Portia was walking my direction. I finished cleaning the glass doors just as she entered the room.

"They're all gone. You need to get out there now and clean that place. Make it spotless. Give him no reason to complain. He'll look for something. Give him nothing. Now go," she said with a wave of her hand. It made me feel like a dog she was shooing away.

I went as commanded to the pool house, disregarding Jasper had said to wait until nine o'clock. He had just left so I figured I was safe. Besides, if Portia continued to treat me like an unwanted pet, I was liable to defend myself and make her angry at me. She didn't want me to be let go. That much was obvious. Again, it made me wonder how she knew my mother, and why she was helping me now. Nineteen years of my life, and not once had I met or even heard of Portia Van Allan.

When I had introduced myself to Portia, I hadn't been brave enough to press or ask for information. At the time, I was grateful that I'd been given the option to take care of Heidi. It was a mystery why the more she did for Heidi and me, the more she worried about Jasper letting me go. It made me wonder what it was my mother had done for Portia to deserve this kind of payment.

The pool was tranquil with the morning sun glistening on its shimmering, dark blue depths. Without the pool area covered in people it was nice out here. Living and working at this house wasn't all that bad. It wasn't home. I didn't feel welcome exactly. But things could be so much worse.

Momma had always told me, "Someone else has it much worse than you. Never feel sorry for yourself. You're alive. That's enough to be thankful for." I had lived by that rule. I still did. It was what kept me sane. It was where I found joy when it seemed there was no reason to be happy. Was my life ideal? No. Was anyone's? No. Everyone had bad things happen. Loss was a part of our walk on this earth.

I resisted the urge to bend down and run my fingers over the smooth surface of the water. Portia was no doubt watching to make sure I went to work like she'd demanded. I hurried to the pool house ready to conquer whatever mess was left for me. I could imagine all kinds of nasty after that party.

When I opened the door to see a perfectly neat living area, I paused. This wasn't nasty at all. Or messy. Sure, the entire place needed some sweeping, mopping, and dusting, but the place wasn't littered with empty beer bottles, food or condoms—which was what I had mentally prepared myself for. I had even expected to find a naked girl lingering.

I hadn't expected a tidy pool house. Not even close.

There was no possible way this place had remained neat during that party. Someone had straightened up. taken out the trash, picked up the dirty towels, and apparently loaded the dishwasher—it was full, but the dishes were clean.

A note written in neat handwriting was on the bar. The list was for grocery items, just like Jasper had said there would be. I didn't expect him to be someone that picked up after himself much less others. This neat freak didn't fit into what I'd thought him to be. I guess I'd been a little judgmental. Jasper Van Allan was a stranger to me. I had no business assuming the worst about him when I didn't know him.

I folded up the list and tucked it into my pocket for later. Then I began pulling out the cleaning supplies that Jasper had told me I'd find under the kitchen sink. The mop and broom would be in the back closet by the bathroom. Surprisingly, the supplies were very organized.

"Jasper said you wouldn't be out here until nine." Winston's voice startled me, causing me to squeal as I spun around holding a spray bottle of cleaner.

"Oh!" was all I managed to say. It was one of those moments where you recognize the voice, but you didn't know they were in the vicinity so you can't help your startled response.

Winston cocked an eyebrow as if he was observing an idiot. I wished I could cock one eyebrow right back at him. "I thought the place was empty," I said defensively.

"And I thought you wouldn't be here until nine," he repeated.

Not that I had to explain myself to him, but I did anyway. "Portia saw Jasper leave and sent me out earlier than anticipated. She wanted me to have plenty time to clean the place." I glanced around. "She obviously expected it to be in much worse shape."

He didn't respond. Instead, he walked to the door and picked up a set of keys that were on the table there. Without a word, he left. Not that he had to tell me goodbye or talk to me at all, but it was rude. Cold even. As if I were not important enough for parting words. *Jerk.*

Jasper was the opposite—he was nice. He wasn't rude. At least not like that. He could be hard at times but I understood he was angry with his mother. To others he seemed fun, polite, kind. Why he was friends with Winston, I had no idea. Nothing about Winston whatever-his-last-name-was remotely resembled Jasper. Except of course, their bank accounts.

I shook him and his behavior from my thoughts. Instead, I focused on my daydreams of going to nursing school one day while I cleaned. I focused on how I would get a job and afford to take care of Heidi on my own. How I would make my mother proud as she watched us from the clouds. All those things kept me humming a tune and enjoying the peace while I worked.

I knew those dreams weren't close. It would take me some

time to figure out the details because all I got paid from Portia was a roof over my head, food, and fifty dollars a week. From that I had to take out the gas money to see Heidi. Portia took care of Heidi's home. That home was the most important thing and all I cared about. But I was only averaging $160 a month in savings. It was going to take years for that to grow into enough money for school tuition, an apartment, and to care for Heidi.

Working nights somewhere was an option I'd been considering. If Portia was okay with my leaving after dinner I could work somewhere a few nights a week. If I could sleep at least three nights a week, I think I could manage it. There weren't a lot of options for night work, but I had been looking around at what was available. The front desk at a hotel, a service station clerk, waitressing at a restaurant, or hostess at a night club. The night club wardrobe wouldn't be great, but that job paid the most. With this being a college town there were several places I could work waiting tables. But a hotel would be so much easier.

It was almost noon when I left for the grocery store. The pool house hadn't taken nearly as long as I thought it would to clean—thanks to Jasper.

Chapter Eight

OVER THE NEXT week, I only saw glimpses of Jasper coming and going from the house. He was always dressed for work. Portia didn't say much, but she watched him as her drinking became regular.

I overheard them one evening while I was doing the laundry. He was raising his voice and accusing her of wasting his money. He was going to start giving her an allowance. She hadn't been happy about that at all.

The next morning she'd woken up and appeared in the kitchen asking for whiskey in her coffee.

When Sunday morning came and there was no notice of guests or another party, I was relieved. I'd be able to attend family day and spend time with Heidi. I had worried all week that I might have to disappoint her again.

I made coffee for Portia—adding the whiskey—then made her a fruit salad using the berries I'd gotten at the store the day before. She never asked for food anymore. I was taking it upon myself to feed her anyway.

She scowled at the fruit, but said nothing as I sat the bowl in front of her. She also didn't mention the whiskey in her coffee. After the argument over money with Jasper, she hadn't talked much at all. I could feel her rage boiling under the surface, though. Each day she was getting worse. I was worried that when she exploded, Jasper and I may both be thrown out.

Today, however, I wasn't going to worry about anything. I took the plate of cookies I had made last night and headed for the back door. When I stepped outside, Jasper was walking from the pool house to the main house. He frowned at the plate of cookies in my hand and at the way I was dressed. This was the only day I wore my own clothing.

"Going somewhere?" he asked.

"Yes," I replied hoping he didn't ask for details.

"Where?"

"It's my day off. Sundays that is. I leave for the morning and most of the afternoon."

He waited as if he wanted more of an explanation. I wasn't sure if I was supposed to tell him more. Portia hadn't told him about Heidi. There had to be a reason why she didn't tell him. I knew that Portia paid for Heidi's care. Now that she was on an allowance and Jasper was taking control of her money, I wasn't sure how that would be affected. He had to know about Heidi and the expense for her care at some point. I worked to provide her that care. It was part of my salary.

"My mother tends to live above her means. She sees no limit to spending. My father never curbed her and she needs to slow down. It isn't her money after all. The amount she has been paying you seems ridiculous. Surely you know that. Six thousand dollars a month is not a normal salary for the job you do here, but Portia was adamant that you needed that much. Regardless, I don't think taking a full day off work on Sunday is fair if you're paid the same amount as some of the executives I know. Do you think I am being unreasonable? If you need Sunday off, I am fine with that. But we need to discuss a new salary. One that makes sense. I don't know anyone who pays a live-in housekeeper that kind of money."

Six thousand dollars? Portia hadn't told me the cost of Heidi's care. I never imagined it was that much every month. I loved where Heidi lived. And she loved it there too, but $6000 was insane. I thought it was around $2500 at most. But never $6000. I wanted that place and the care Heidi was being given, but how could I ask the Van Allen's to pay that? He was right of course. My job and salary wasn't worth even half that a month.

"I . . ." I had no idea what to say. Words didn't come. If I took Sunday's off and he lowered my pay that meant Heidi would have to leave the home. She'd adjusted to her life and was happy. How could I jerk her out and move her somewhere else?

I'd have to work nights to make it work. Not to save for college, but to pay for her to stay at the home. I could not expect Jasper to continue my over-the-top salary because Heidi needed special care.

Jasper was right. It wasn't fair at all.

"Okay," I finally said. "What is fair?" I should discuss this with him in more depth, but I didn't know what else to say.

"I asked around this week after I saw how much you were getting paid a month. The average for your job is $2800 with room and board. Ms. Charlotte was being paid three thousand when she retired and that was after sixteen years of working here. Considering you've been paid $6000 for the past six months I would hope you've saved up money. I think the fair thing to do here is pay you $2000 for the next six months to even out some of the exorbitant pay you've been receiving. This job can be harder at times. I'll have more parties. There will be more entertaining that you'll be responsible for. But you have been paid well. I expect you see that. Portia gave you that salary and like anyone else would, you accepted it. Can't say I blame you. But it was too much. Entirely over the top."

Two thousand. I'd need to somehow make $4000 more a month to keep Heidi at the home. How would I do that? It seemed impossible. All I could do was nod my head. I couldn't argue with him. It wasn't his responsibility to take care of my sister. He didn't have to give me a job and he owed me nothing. Portia had felt some form of payment was meant for my mother, although I have no idea why. But Jasper knew as little about that as me.

"We are clear then. You are free to take your Sunday's off. Starting at the first of the month your paycheck will be $2000."

I nodded again. It was all I could do.

He gave me a tight smile. "Glad we can agree. You handle Portia well. She wants to keep you. That's not easy to manage because she's hard to please. I have no fault with your job. You do it well. No complaints. But I would like to add some things to your job description. Starting with having breakfast on the table for me at eight every morning. I'll leave a list of things I prefer and I take my coffee black and strong. I also want my bedding changed every three days and my sheets should be pressed. I need you to keep my fridge stocked with the items I will also list. Check it daily, and make sure I'm not running low on anything. I am sure I will have a few more things to add. But we can discuss that later.

For now, go enjoy your day off," he said ending our conversation with a friendly smile this time.

Then he reached under the plastic wrap on the plate I was carrying and took a cookie. "I like cookies too. Leaving me some would be appreciated." With that he walked into the main house.

I couldn't move just yet. My stomach was in knots and my thoughts raced with how I'd make up the difference of that money. How would I take care of Heidi now? Would I be able to keep her in the place she was now calling home?

I turned to see Portia standing inside watching me. Her face was blank, lacking any emotional. She was simply staring my way.

Would she tell Jasper about Heidi? Was that even an issue? He had no reason to take care of my sister or give me a job. He was giving me a place to live and work. Heidi lived only ten miles from here. I had to find a way to make this work. The only answer was for me to get a second job. One where I could make the most money.

I'd have to leave Heidi early today to find out if any clubs were hiring nineteen year olds. A club would pay the best, even if all I could do was work as a hostess. The college clubs let nineteen year olds in with a band on their wrist marking them as too young to drink. I was pretty sure I could get a job at a club or maybe as a waitress somewhere.

For now, I had to visit my sister and smile. And pretend it was okay. That our lives weren't holding on by a thread yet again.

Chapter Nine

THE BRIGHT LIGHTS outside Rocks on The Riverfront—an eighteen-year-old and older club that was located on the roof of a well-known hotel—seemed to be highlighting it as the most popular location for the college crowd in the area.

I had left Heidi at four that afternoon and spent an hour searching for places that were hiring and were open late night or all night. Rocks on The Riverfront didn't get busy until nine in the evenings, and was open until three in the morning. Those were perfect hours for me.

It wasn't even seven yet. I'd called asking if they were hiring, and a girl had me speak to Mr. Carey Jones, the manager. He said he'd interview me at the club at seven o'clock. Mr. Jones went on to tell me that they had limited positions for someone my age, but he may have an opening for a hostess. I knew without him saying anything he wanted to see what I looked like. My appearance mattered at a place like this. I hated that, but I was desperate.

The short black skirts and tight black halter tops the girls were wearing when I walked in were expected, but seeing the uniform only made me more nervous. I never dressed like that. The most revealing thing I owned was cut-off blue jean shorts. This would be difficult to adjust to. If it paid enough that I could pay for Heidi's care, I could live with it.

"We don't open for another thirty minutes," a redheaded girl with long-in-no-way-natural eyelashes said as she stopped in front of me. No one else seemed to notice me until her.

"I'm here to meet with Carey Jones," I told her.

She did a quick scan of my appearance and nodded. "Of course. This way."

Her hips swayed when she walked and the short skirt she wore barely covered her bottom. I imagined that got her a lot of tips. She was probably paying for her college. Or maybe she had someone she had to take care of too.

"He's in there. Knock and wait. He'll answer when he's done."

"Thank you," I told her, grateful she had stopped to help me.

"Yep," was all she said in return before leaving me standing outside Mr. Jones's office.

I knocked on the door and waited. I heard voices inside, and I didn't want to be rude by knocking again, but I wondered if they hadn't heard me. One voice sounded female and made a high-pitched noise that sounded a little . . . Odd to be coming from the office.

Before I knocked again, someone came to a stop beside me.

"You looking for Carey?" a tall guy with brown hair pulled back in a ponytail and bright green eyes asked.

"Yes."

He nodded then knocked loudly on the door. "You got

company!" he yelled, then looked back at me. "Give them a minute to get dressed," he said as he turned and walked down the hall.

If I hadn't been nervous before, I was now. They were getting dressed. Which meant they hadn't been dressed. Which meant the high-pitched squeal I'd heard was exactly that—a high-pitched *sex* squeal. Maybe his girlfriend worked here. I had no problem with sex in the workplace. I just thought it was weird when Mr. Jones knew he had an interview about now.

The door finally opened and a tall, leggy woman with platinum blonde hair walked out. She ran her hand over her mussed hair and sauntered past me without even a glance.

"Come on in," the man inside said. I took a deep breath and entered the office.

I'd had sex only once in my life. It hadn't been enjoyable and I hadn't tried it again since. But I wasn't innocent. I had been to parties in high school. I'd been around sex. I knew what it smelled like. And this office smelled strongly of sex.

Carey Jones didn't appear to notice, or he didn't care.

He ran his hand through his thinning hair and gave me a once over much the same way the redhead had.

"You're uh," he glanced down at a piece of paper on his desk that looked creased from being sat on. "Beulah?" he said, then looked back up at me.

"Yes sir."

He grinned then. "Nice. You can read, write, and walk in heels, correct?"

Those were odd questions. "Yes."

"When can you start?"

"Uh, as soon as possible."

"Good. Tonight's not a good night for training. Monday nights are slower to learn the ropes. Be here at tomorrow night at eight. I'll have a uniform waiting for you. Size four?"

I nodded not sure if this was a joke or just this easy.

"I've got to handle a mistake with some ordering at the bar. So, unless you have any questions, take this application and consent form with you. Fill them out. Bring them with you tomorrow— and I'll need a copy of your driver's license."

"Okay," I said, taking the papers from him. Then I realized I had no idea what the pay was. If this would even be enough. "Do you know how many hours a week I'll be working and what I will make an hour?"

"I can work you as many as forty hours a week and as few as twenty-five. Your call. And hostess is paid twelve dollars an hour. You don't get tips like the servers so the pay is better. However, many times my hostesses get tipped for putting customers in the spots they want. That kind of thing. So, there is a way to make more."

This wasn't going to be enough, but where else could I get twelve dollars an hour? "Okay. Thank you," I answered. He gave me a creepy wide grin before leaving me in his office.

I walked out of his office with the papers in my hand. After taxes, I would make about $1500 a month. That's working forty hours a week. I needed more money. Or I could talk to someone at Among the Spanish Moss about a payment plan until I could figure out how to make more money. Maybe I could get Heidi a smaller room, if that was even an option. I had no idea. Portia had handled everything with the home.

I'd been so relieved to have somewhere for Heidi that wasn't a cardboard box on the street snuggled up next to me that I hadn't asked. Now, I needed to know. I had to figure this out. I should have been figuring this out from the start. Not just assuming Portia would always take care of things. I didn't have the excuse of losing Mom anymore. I'd mourned her. I'd cried myself to sleep many nights. I had to grow up now. She'd would have expected me to.

This job was going to be exhausting. I wouldn't have time to work three jobs. These two would take all my time. Tomorrow, I'd call and talk to the people at Among the Spanish Moss and see what could be done. If I had to, I'd find another home for Heidi. It would upset her and that would break my heart. But if it was impossible to keep her there, I didn't know what else to do. She couldn't be left alone while I worked and there was nowhere I'd make the money I had been making with the Van Allan's.

Someone, somewhere, was having a harder time than me. I could overcome this. I could make this work. I would not feel sorry for myself. Tonight, I may cry just a little. Then I'd be tough.

Chapter Ten

PORTIA WAS SITTING in the great room when I got home after eight o'clock. She looked at me with the same expression she'd had earlier. She hadn't expected any of this when she'd been looking forward to Jasper's visit. I wondered if she wished he'd never come. I imagine that was what she thought about most of the time now.

"What will you do?" she asked me when I entered the room. She didn't look at me. She kept her gaze fixed on her manicured nails.

"I'm going to work nights. I got a job working at a club. That still won't cover the place she's at, but I am going to talk to them about a cheaper room or possible payments."

"She can share a room for four thousand a month," Portia said lifting her head to look at me. "But that is still a lot. More than you can manage. How long do you think you can work two jobs? What happens when he has late parties and you have to work?"

I hadn't thought of that. It would be a problem. I wasn't sure how I could manage this. "Are we keeping Heidi a secret from him on purpose?" I asked. "Not that he should feel obligated to help me pay for her care, but maybe he would understand my need for a second job?"

She shrugged. "I don't know with him. His father was a cold man. He had no heart. No emotion. Often, he was cruel. I married him young and fresh off the farm. So sure I'd live this fairy-tale life I'd always wanted. The one I thought I should have been born into. I saw glittery things, luxury, and I wanted it all. But with it came a price. He changed me. I changed," she looked away from me.

Her gaze was now focused on the portrait that hung over the mantel. It was Jasper. A much younger Jasper. "He's so much like his father. He can be charming, but he's cold. I can't trust his actions. I've helped you all I can, and feel that I did my duty. You're not mine to worry over. Your mother knew that and she sent you here anyway. It's up to you now, so figure it out. This is your life. I have my own to deal with."

I stood there not sure what to say. There was nothing to say after that really.

There was only one question I didn't know the answer to. "Why did you help us to begin with then?"

She stood up. The linen pants she was wearing were now wrinkled from her sitting there for too long. She still managed to look elegant. "Because. I owed your mother for something that happened long ago. I've done my duty. If there is a God and he does care about our souls, I think he'll agree I fulfilled what was expected of me."

I can't say any of what she said made sense. I wanted more

of an explanation. "But what did you owe my mother?"

Portia sighed as if she'd been wearied by my presence. "Nothing. Not really. She made a choice that led to where you are today. That's not my problem to fix. But she is gone now. I did a kind act for the dead. Nothing more."

She left the room before I could say more. *A kind act for the dead?* That was all this was? There had been moments when Portia seemed to care. That she worried about Heidi and me. But now I wondered if I had imagined those moments. That I'd made them up in my head. *Wishful thinking.*

I left the room the way I had entered. This wasn't my home. It never had been. Portia wasn't family. My sister was my only family now. Allowing myself to think there was a chance Portia cared for us had been a mistake. It made me vulnerable. I couldn't be vulnerable. I had to be strong. Tough. Figure this out. Because Portia was right about one thing: it was my problem. Not hers, and definitely not Jasper's. Telling him my situation would be asking for help, and I wasn't doing that.

The doors that led to the veranda opened. I stopped and turned around to see Jasper and Winston walking inside. Jasper was talking and stopped when he saw me.

"Hello. I hope you enjoyed your day off." He sounded sincere.

"I did. Thank you."

"We're here to find food. Not much of a cook and I'm tired of eating easy things out there just to avoid my mother. Could you make us something to eat? Stone was going to, but you're here and I imagine you could make something tastier than what he can throw together."

Stone? Who was Stone?

"Uh, sure. Any requests? Or do you want me to just make

something?"

Jasper looked at Winston. "You were going to make fettucine with alfredo sauce, right? You want that or you want her to make something else?"

Winston was Stone? How had I missed that?

"I'm good with whatever. Provided she can cook," he said not looking at me or acknowledging my presence. Once again, I felt like I'd been transported to the Victorian era and I was the servant around him.

Jasper chuckled. "Ignore him. He's a bit of a dick. You just fix something. I'm so hungry I don't care what it is. Just no grilled cheese. I've made myself sick of those."

I nodded. "I'll get right to it."

"Do you know if my mother has gone up to her room?" Jasper called out as I walked away.

"Yes. I believe so."

He let out a sigh of relief. "Good. Not in the mood to listen to her bitch."

I didn't reply, I just exited. I would talk to Jasper later about my second job. I was going to use my excuse for saving for college as the reason why. For now, Heidi would remain a secret. I didn't want to appear to be asking for his help. That wasn't the case. I just needed his understanding. Money for college sounded believable enough. Besides, only last week, that was what I had been planning to do. It wasn't a complete lie. Not really.

I stood in the kitchen and looked at the pantry. I wanted to make something impressive after Mr. Snooty Pants made that comment about my cooking ability. I decided I'd go with what I knew from home—my favorite meal momma made. Homemade biscuits, bacon, sausage gravy and cheese grits. It was breakfast food, but on special occasions momma made it at night. We loved when she did. Homemade biscuits were always good. Smiling, I reached for the supplies I'd need and got to work.

The smell of the biscuits in the oven and the bacon frying filled the kitchen pretty quickly. I smiled to myself. I was sure there wasn't a Southern boy alive who wouldn't like this meal. I felt confident they'd both enjoy it, and Winston or Stone or whoever would have to eat his words. *Jerk.*

By the time I finished the cheese grits and was finishing the gravy, the door swung open and Jasper walked inside. "That smells fucking incredible. Are you making breakfast? I know I smell bacon."

I didn't let him see the grin that I was struggling to hide as it spread across my face. "Yep."

"I love bacon," he told me.

"Most people do," I agreed.

He stood watching me, and I finished up without filling the silence with small talk. He was my boss. I didn't figure he expected that from me.

"Look. About our talk earlier today, I didn't mean to sound harsh if I did. I am just trying to fix the things my mother has handled poorly."

I nodded. I didn't need any more explanation. He had every right to question me being paid that much.

"I know today was your day off so thanks for this. I shouldn't have asked you to cook. I'm sure you had something else you wanted to do."

I reached for two plates in the cabinet. "I was going to do laundry and read. I still plan on it. It's early. Do you want me to serve y'all or do you want to just make your own plates and eat in here? Wasn't sure if this was a casual thing or not."

He took the plates from my hand. "We can fix our plates and eat in here. No need for the big ass dining room table in there. We can even use paper towels instead of the monogramed napkins Portia has us use."

Stone walked in then. "Is that bacon?"

I smiled. I couldn't help myself. I'd accomplished what I wanted.

"She made us breakfast," Jasper replied.

Stone didn't look pleased or disappointed. He looked like he always did. No emotion. Dark and closed off. I knew he could smile, though. I'd seen it that one time. It was just when I was around he didn't smile. I wasn't sure why he didn't like me unless he just didn't like any of the hired help.

"If y'all are good, then I'll leave y'all to it," I told Jasper.

"Yeah. This is great. Enjoy your evening. And your book."

I gave him a parting smile, then left. I didn't look at Winston. There was no point. He pretended I didn't exist anyway.

Chapter Eleven

I HAD PLANNED on talking to Jasper about my second job today. But he was gone before I could catch him. When dinner came and went and there was still no sign of him, I was out of time. Dressing in a pair of shorts and T-shirt of my own, I headed upstairs to tell Portia I would be at work tonight, but that I'd be back in time to make breakfast.

She had been gone most of the day with her friends at a tennis match. The farro and kale salad I'd made her for dinner had seemed to please her, but she didn't say much. She used to enjoy bossing me around and complaining. Now she didn't seem to enjoy much of anything.

I finally found her downstairs at the bar pouring herself a drink. "You're leaving. Does he know?" she said without turning around to look at me.

"No. I never got a chance to tell him."

She sighed and took a drink as she turned around. "If he

comes home and needs something from you, what do you expect me to say?"

I had no idea what she should say. I didn't expect her to say anything.

"I don't know. I'll explain tomorrow."

"If you still have a job tomorrow," she said flippantly, walking past me out of the room.

I couldn't worry about that right now. Yes, this job paid more but it wouldn't be enough. I had to work another job. The house was clean, the pool house was clean, groceries were stocked in both places. I even left him a warm dinner at the pool house in case he was hungry when he got home. That was all I could do.

I pulled my purse higher on my shoulder and headed out the back door toward the parking spot where I was allowed to keep my car.

"Leaving? You have more off time than I'd expect considering your salary."

I paused and closed my eyes tightly. I couldn't tell Stone off. He was Jasper's friend. I had to deal with him. He'd also tell Jasper I had left, so I needed to give him an explanation. One I hoped would be given to Jasper properly.

"I just got a second job. I've completed all my duties for today. I planned on talking to Jasper about my second job, but he was gone this morning before I had a chance."

Stone looked at me. Which was rare. "A second job? What, they aren't paying you enough now? You have a free place to live, food and a ridiculous sum of money and you think you need to work a second job? That's not exactly believable. Lying to Jasper won't benefit you."

I really hated him. He was a dark, beautiful, cruel man. Why

was he always here? Didn't he have a job, or was he just living off
his daddy's money?

"It isn't a lie. I can prove it to him if I need to. Now if you'll
excuse me, I don't believe I have to discuss my income with you."
I walked past him and into the darkness toward my car.

I was not looking forward to tonight. I was nervous and hoped
I could do this job. I wasn't even sure what would be expected of
me. I hadn't been given much of a job description.

Once I was in my car and driving away, I breathed a sigh of
relief. I was almost worried that Stone would follow me out to
my car, continuing his intrusive questioning. If Jasper wanted
details and proof I'd give it to him. But Stone wasn't my boss.
He was nothing.

The drive to the club was only thirteen minutes without
much traffic. If it had been two hours earlier, this drive would
have taken an hour. But going to work at eight in the evening
had a few advantages. I'd cleaned and grocery shopped all day
so my feet hurt and I just wanted to take a shower and sit down.
Or lie down. That wasn't going to be happening anytime soon,
though. I had to work for the next seven hours. The idea made
me even more exhausted. I had to picture Heidi's smile to give
me the strength to park the car and head into my new work place.

The first person I saw when I walked in the front doors was
the redhead from last night who had taken me to Carey's office.
She waved me over to her. "I need to get you a uniform. Then
Neil will be showing you the ropes tonight. You can shadow
him—and take notes."

"Okay," I said hurrying to follow her down the same hallway
I'd been in last night that led to Carey's office.

We passed his door and went all the way to the end. A blue

door that said Employees Only was to our right. The redhead opened it and we went inside. There were uniforms on hangers along the back wall and dressing rooms. There were also mirrors, toilets and one shower.

"This is where we dress, use the facilities, and take breaks," she said as she walked to the uniforms and took one from the rack. "A four correct?"

I nodded.

"Put this on." She reached down and picked up a pair of red high heels that had sparkly toes. "Wear these."

"I need an eight," I told her not wanting to have to squeeze my foot into yet another shoe.

She sat them down and picked up another pair. "Here. They run small. These are nines."

The idea of walking around in heels didn't seem so bad now that I knew my toes weren't going to be cramped all night. "Thank you."

"Sure. Get dressed and then come out to the front. Neil will be waiting on you."

"Who's Neil?"

She paused at the door. "Tall guy. Dark blonde hair. He will be looking for you. Just head out front."

"Okay," I replied as she walked out. I still didn't know her name. She wasn't exactly the friendly sort.

I got busy changing into the work uniform, and then stood in front of the full-length mirror and winced. The skirt was so short I was afraid to bend over. I'd have to watch that tonight. Slipping on the heels I felt more vulnerable than I ever had, like I was on display. I didn't like attention. This outfit was going to get me attention.

I could always keep looking for another good paying evening job. This didn't have to be forever. It wasn't like I was the only one dressed this way. There were other servers who would be just as scantily dressed, and more than likely, so would the customers. This was a club. I had to get over myself.

After I gave myself a pep talk, I made my way down the hallway toward the front where Neil would be waiting on me. The first person I saw was the guy who had met me outside Carey's office last night and knocked on his door. He was tall with dark blonde hair. When he saw me, he waved me over. It was the guy I was supposed to trail, Neil. Or at least I assumed he was.

"Beulah, correct?" he asked holding out his hand. "I'm Neil."

"Yes, and it's nice to officially meet you," I told him.

He smirked. "Yeah, I was in a hurry last night or I'd have been friendlier."

"That's fine. I thought you were friendly enough."

He ran his hand through his hair and glanced around the place. People were trickling in, but it wasn't busy yet. "This is the early crowd. They are here to eat the bar food and do some socializing before the crowd. A Monday night crowd isn't that bad. It's the slowest night of the week for us. That's why Carey had you come in so soon to start. This is the night he likes to train his newbies."

Neil pointed at the redhead. "That's Shauna. She's the manager of the waitresses and hostesses. She's been here for five years. She's not the nicest person around, but she works hard and makes sure the place runs smooth."

He began to walk and I followed. "If you need something, come to me first. Shauna doesn't like dealing with the little details. She deals with the big issues. I am second in command and I deal with the small stuff. If it's too much for me to smooth over,

I involve her. She's big on the chain of command thing, so don't go directly to her unless I tell you to. She looks pretty but she can go monster on you in a second."

We walked to the hostess area, and he patted the countertop that stood between me and guests as they arrived. "If the guests get to you, then they made it through security. They will have on blue bracelets that have our logo on them if they are under twenty-one. You will greet them, take any bags, wraps or jackets—which won't be many this time of year—and check them in. Tag their item with a number using these tickets, then give them the other half. Put their items in that room. In the winter, this is a busier job. Much more of a hassle and we have three people working the front then because of it. Right now, it won't be a big deal. With me so far? Any questions?"

This seemed easy enough so far. My nerves had eased and I nodded. "Yes, I am good. What else?"

"Fast learner. I like it. Okay, you will look at this chart and decide on what table, section area to seat them. If they have paid for VIP reservations, you will have them stand here away from the crowd, and contact me or whoever is on duty handling the VIP. We will seat them. You don't handle them—you handle the rest."

The next few hours went on like this. I followed Neil around and he never stopped talking. He was constantly teaching me something. I even took a few shopping bags and one silk wrap and tagged them in the coat check. When two in the morning rolled around, the place was almost empty and I was told I could leave.

Sinking into the front seat of my car, I slipped off my heels and stretched. *I can do this.*

I touched the hidden pocket on my skirt. There was fifty dollars in there from customers who had tipped me. The lady with the silk wrap had given me a twenty-dollar bill when I returned her wrap to her. The other thirty dollars came from a group of guys I seated. Neil said if they tipped me, to be thankful and take it. So, I did.

Chapter Twelve

T HE THREE AND a half hours I slept last night felt like I barely closed my eyes. The alarm went off by my head, and for a moment I thought I was at home in in our single-wide trailer. I was still in bed, it was a school morning and I was going to hit the snooze button. But when I peeled my eyes open to find the blasted noisy alarm, I saw the washing machine and I remembered I wasn't home. I wasn't in school anymore.

Yawning, I stretched and my calves burned. My feet ached, and my eyes felt raw as if I had cried all night. But I hadn't. I laid there and stared at the ceiling. It was a fancy ceiling for a basement. It was white with crown molding. Much like the rest of the house.

I wondered how many mornings Ms. Charlotte had laid here and stared at that ceiling. Had she ever wished to quit? Or had she loved working here? I couldn't imagine loving working for the Van Allan's. They weren't a happy bunch.

I also wondered if her shoes had fit her as I wiggled my

toes, dreading putting on my shoes. Lying here wasn't going to get breakfast cooked nor was it going to give me time to catch Jasper before he left today. I had to talk to him. There was a good chance Stone already had. When I'd gotten in last night and my code for the door still worked, I thought that was a positive sign. At least I hadn't been kicked out.

With great reluctance, I crawled out of bed and got dressed. I left putting on my shoes for last, just before I went upstairs. The good news was I didn't have to chase Jasper down this morning. He was already awake and in the kitchen. The bad news was he appeared to be waiting on me to arrive and he wasn't smiling. The coffee in his hand said he hadn't just arrived. It was only six-thirty, and I'd never seen him up this early. Another negative.

"Good morning," I said, stopping after I walked into the room. I didn't know what to expect but I was prepared. I would be more prepared if I'd had my coffee, but I was prepared enough. This was a conversation I'd gone over in my head several times the past twenty-four hours.

"Late night?" he asked, and then took a sip of his coffee.

"Yes. I'm guessing Winston told you about my second job."

He frowned. "Second job?"

Oh. So Stone hadn't told him. Oops. That wasn't the way I wanted ed to lead into it.

"You need a second job? I thought you were paid very well here. Surely there isn't anything that costs so much in your life you need more money."

This was where I considered telling him about Heidi. It would be easier. It would make sense. But I was scared. I had watched people mistreat her over and over in the past. They didn't want the hassle, or they didn't understand. Could I trust Jasper with something this important?

"I'm saving to attend college." There. That had been the truth once. Didn't make it the truth now, but I didn't know Jasper well enough to trust him.

"Really? What do you want to major in?"

"Nursing. I want to go to Nursing school."

He looked inside his coffee mug, and then set it down on the counter. "That's why you need a second job? You're still making two grand a month. You made thirty-six thousand over the past six months. I don't imagine nursing school costs that much up front."

"I wanted to be sure I could complete school. Pay for it in full."

He didn't seem satisfied. "What nursing school do you want to attend? I would think in just a couple more months you'd have your complete tuition just working here. You have no rent, bills, or food to pay for. I assume you own that car—it's not anywhere near new. What have you been spending your money on? Do you have some addiction I need to know about? You don't look the part, but the dark circles under your eyes and the way you were dressed when came home night was questionable."

He'd seen me come home? I hadn't seen him. That was why he was up early waiting on me. Stone hadn't told him anything. Which was odd. I'd expected him to.

"That was my uniform. I don't get to choose what I wear. As for the circles, I'm tired but I will adjust. I don't have nor have I ever had any form of addiction."

Maybe it was my exhaustion. Maybe it was the fear he wouldn't believe me, but for whatever reason, I decided it was time for the truth. All I could hope was that he would understand and didn't end up tossing me out, accusing me of mooching off his mother. If I told him about Heidi and he didn't accept she needed to be taken care at the home, then I'd just leave. I would work three jobs if I had to.

"I have a sister," I said knowing I couldn't turn back now. I had to tell him everything. I'd admit it and deal with the outcome. I wasn't asking for a hand out. I wasn't hoping to get more money out of Portia. I'd come here simply because my mother had told me to. I had no other choice.

"Okay, I assume you have a family. What has that got to do with this?"

"She's my only family. All I have left. Our mother died of pneumonia six months ago." I paused.

"I'm listening," he said waiting on me to continue.

I took a deep breath and let it out. I was nervous. This could be a mistake. But I was tired of keeping this a secret when it wasn't something I should have to keep a secret. It wasn't bad. It wasn't illegal. It was my life. Simple as that.

"Heidi. That's her name. She got the better name. She was born second. I'm the oldest by three minutes."

"You have a twin?" he asked, raising his eyebrows in surprise. "I was expecting you to tell me you had a little sister that you had to support. Wasn't expecting a twin."

I bit my bottom lip and looked away. The next part I had to tell him was the most important. It was what made me strong yet vulnerable at the same time. Heidi was my strength, yet taking care of her was where all my fear came from. What if I couldn't? What if I failed her?

"She's . . . special. The most special person I've ever known. She has been the one person in my life to always bring a smile to my face. To remind me how there is always something in life to be happy about. That joy can come from a single hug. Heidi and I aren't identical. Not just that, but I was born normal. She wasn't. Heidi has Down syndrome."

He didn't say anything. We stood there in the kitchen in silence and it felt like a massive weight was sitting on my chest as I waited for him to say something. Or maybe I needed to say more? To continue explaining.

"Where is she now?"

"A home your mother put her in when I came here after our mother's death. It's called Among the Spanish Moss. I didn't want to put Heidi in a home but I can't work and take care of her. She needs constant supervision and our mother did that every day until I got home from school. Then she worked evenings while I took care of Heidi. When I came here your mother gave me a job and put Heidi in a wonderful place. They are good to her there and she has friends. But, it's not cheap."

Jasper's forehead was pinched in a deep frown. "Portia was paying for Heidi's care? That was where all the money was going?"

I nodded.

His frown remained. I felt my stomach knot up.

"Sundays . . . you leave here to see her, don't you?"

I nodded again.

"The cookies," he let out a laugh that held no humor. "And I thought you'd made them for some guy."

"She likes cookies. And so does the staff there. I like to take them treats."

He sighed and leaned back against the counter crossing his arms over his chest. "How much does the place cost a month?"

"It was six thousand. But I'm having her moved to a shared room which will decrease it to four thousand. She likes company. If I'd even known that was an option in the beginning I would have asked for that. But Portia had arranged everything and I had no clue. I was so grateful I didn't question her. I also had no idea how much she was paying until this past week. Our deal was I worked and she gave me fifty dollars a week for gas and any other needs. The rest of my pay was to take care of Heidi. There were other places she could have put Heidi. I know I could find a more affordable home but she loves the people there. She's adjusted. Losing mom was harder on her because she didn't understand. Moving her from the only home she had known to live with strangers had been a huge adjustment for her. The idea of doing it again breaks my heart. I do not expect you to pay for that of course. I agree with you that it was too much. Especially now that I know how much it is. But if I could be allowed to work the second job, it will help."

He didn't say anything at first. I waited. I'd said all I could say.

"One last question. Why did you come here? To Portia?"

I wasn't sure if Portia wanted him to know this part or not. But I was in too deep now. I had to confess everything. "My mother gave me a piece of paper with Portia's name and address the day before she died. She was so sick. Her fever was high and she was delirious. She said the hospital bill would break us and refused to go. I thought she'd be fine at home, that she only had a bad cold. Then the coughing got worse. When she gave me the name and number and told me that if something happened to her to call that lady, I got scared.

When she went to sleep that night, I called 9–1–1. They came and took her and she was admitted to the hospital. But it was too late. She was too far gone. The day after her funeral, the landlord told me we were behind two months on rent. He hated to do it, but if we didn't pay he'd have to evict us. I packed up our things and we came here, not knowing what to expect. Portia looked at the note, and asked us to come inside. The next day Heidi was moved into her new home. I began work."

I could see Jasper was questioning who my mother was and why Portia would help her. I did too. Maybe he could find it out because I'd had no luck. He didn't appear angry though. Just lost in thought. Portia had been there when I needed her. I felt guilty telling him what had happened. It felt like I had turned on her. Not asked her for permission. She should have been warned, I owed her that.

"I know you and your mother have a strained relationship. But she was there for us when we had no one. I should have talked to her before I told you everything. It's not fair that I didn't."

His lips tugged up in an almost smile. "Do you worry about everyone, Beulah Edwards?"

"No. Not anymore than anyone else does."

He laughed softly and shook his head. "I'd question that—did I just listen to you explain your life? You're incredibly naïve. You can keep your second job. Portia isn't in trouble."

I sighed, relieved he was understanding. "Thank you. Can I make you breakfast now?"

The almost smile stayed in place and he picked up his coffee cup and handed it to me. "I make shit coffee. Can you make me some? Yours is better. And I'd like something to eat. I'm up early, so I'll get dressed and come back."

I took his cup and watched him leave. For the first time he arrived here, I didn't feel fear clawing at my neck.

Chapter Thirteen

JASPER WAS FINISHING breakfast when Stone walked into the house. He was dressed in worn out jeans and a black T-shirt. I'd never seen him dress up like Jasper. He left every day, but I didn't think it was for work.

"She makes damn good waffles. She puts some fruit cream stuff on them and there are strawberries inside," Jasper told Stone as I took his plate.

"Sounds delicious," he said with no enthusiasm.

"Could you bring one of those things for my charming friend here?" Jasper said with a roll of his eyes.

"Of course," I replied and turned to Stone. "Can I get you coffee?"

He didn't look at me, but nodded. "Juice too. Orange. Fresh squeezed."

I left with Jasper's plate before they began talking. I wondered if he would tell Jasper about my second job this morning. Maybe he had been waiting until it was awkward for me. That fit him. To be cruel.

I'd made several waffles, unsure who I would be feeding. So the only thing that took any time preparing Winston's meal was squeezing the oranges in the juicer. Once I had his freshly squeezed juice, I carried his breakfast to the table.

"You're going to have to discuss it with him sooner or later," Jasper was saying as I walked back in.

"I didn't ask you," Stone replied.

Jasper smirked and turned his attention to me. "He's always such a joy. Have you noticed that?"

I didn't say anything. I didn't even smile. I placed his food in front of him and stood back to see if there was anything else they needed.

"I plan on staying around this morning and speaking with Portia. If you'd like to be present I'm fine with that."

I paused then. He was going to talk to her about Heidi and me? Why she helped us? That meant he'd possibly get the answers I had been curious about myself. Not that I wasn't thankful for all she'd done, but because she knew my mother. She knew her once and I wanted to know how. I missed my mother and had no one to talk to about her. No friends to remember her with. Bringing her up when I was with Heidi always confused her. I had tried that once and it hadn't gone well.

If Portia knew momma and could talk with me about her, I wanted that. I wanted anything Portia could offer. Any link to her. "I'd like that," I told him.

Stone stopped mid-bite, his fork almost to his mouth. "What did I miss?"

Jasper looked at me and it was as if unspoken words were

exchanged. With just a look I understood his question and he understood my answer. I'd never experienced that before. "Just Portia being Portia. I need to lay down some rules for her to follow regarding Beulah—she also works for me. Mother isn't remembering that is all."

Stone turned his gaze to me and I saw the accusation in his eyes. He thought I had lied about my job. That I was hiding it. I had the urge to defend myself but I didn't. What he thought of me didn't matter.

"Meet me in the great room at ten. She'll be in her whiskey by then I'm sure," he said.

I nodded my head once, then left the room.

"You've got your own shit to deal with. Jesus, the drama. Stay out of mine," I heard Stone say to him.

Jasper chuckled. "But yours is more fun to discuss."

"Because you like to pretend your life is fucking peaches."

"My life has never been peaches. But then neither has yours. Now, tell me. Has your mother picked out the engagement ring she intends for you to give Margot?"

Whoever Margot was, I felt sympathy for her. No amount of good looks and money could make living with Stone a pleasant thing. But he hadn't mentioned my job. That was surprising. I had expected he wanted to get me in trouble. It seemed to be his way of doing things.

Thinking about that and poor Margot was pointless. I pushed it aside and thought of other things. Like how many nights I could go without sleeping only three hours before I crashed. I made myself a thermos of coffee and carried it with me as I went to the second floor to do the weekly dusting and changing of linens for beds that no one ever slept in.

The only real thing needed on that floor was dusting and the floors had to be swept. Everything else stayed spotless because no one was ever up there. Portia's master suite was on the third floor. I only went up there when she was gone for the day. She liked her privacy.

The next three hours passed by swiftly, and I was checking my watch every ten minutes waiting for ten o'clock to arrive. The idea Portia might be able to tell me something about my mother might not seem like a big deal, but to me it meant so much. Anything to understand why she'd sent us here. A small piece of her past. To hear her talked about again.

At ten, I put the cleaning supplies away and made my way to the great room. My eyes locked with Jasper's as I entered and he gave me a small smile. It wasn't much, but it was encouraging. Like I wasn't alone and he was my friend. I knew that wasn't the case, but it felt like it.

"Why is she here? I assume this is about her other job. Yes, I knew, and if you have a problem with it then deal with it yourself." Portia didn't even glance my way. "I need my coffee, Beulah. Where have you been?"

Jasper cleared his throat and got my attention then motioned for me to take a seat. "Please Beulah, ignore her and sit down."

Portia's head snapped up from the iPad in her lap that she'd been studying. "What?"

"I want to talk to you. I have questions. I feel that Beulah should be in here for this. Now, let's begin with how you knew Beulah's mother. You and I both know you don't have a kind bone in your body. So why did you so willingly help these two girls?"

Portia's gaze swung to me. "You told him?"

"I had to. He needed to understand why I was working a

second job."

She sighed dramatically and slung her iPad down on the sofa beside her with obvious disgust. "I help you and this is the thanks I get. Do you understand that he could take all that back? Demand a refund? Are you that dense girl?"

I didn't know how to respond to that. I stilled and waited, dropping my gaze from hers to study my hands.

"Father left me this house, the money, the investments, and the corporation. His will stated that I was to do with you whatever I pleased. If I chose to take care of you, fine. If not, you'd find another man to leech off. So, mother, I'd be more careful how you speak to Beulah. All she did was tell me what you should have already explained. Since it was my money that was helping Heidi, I'd like to know why you did it. What do you owe Beulah and Heidi's mother? Because you don't do things out of the kindness of your heart. There must be something you're hiding. I need to know what that is."

Portia glared at me. I could feel it burning through me where I stood. But I didn't look up. I felt guilty. She'd helped me, and now here I sat with Jasper who was talking to her in a way I didn't think was necessary, demanding she answer questions. I wasn't here when he was growing up. I didn't know the kind of mother that Portia was, but from the anger and bitterness in her son's tone, I imagined it hadn't been a happy home.

"I knew Pamela many years ago. She made some bad choices and went a different way in life. I don't owe her a damn thing. No one does. She had passed away and I felt a connection and pity for the life she'd lived. She had so much potential when I knew her. But she," Portia paused and I lifted my eyes to finally look at her. "She was stupid. Naïve. It got her nowhere. I was kind to a woman I once knew. That was all. I feel like I did my duty and whatever you choose to do with Beulah's employment is fine with me. She's had plenty of time to figure out a way to take care of Heidi and herself. She's almost twenty. Past time she grew up."

Nothing more than what she'd already said to me before. No explanation. No real connection to my mother, but my mother had known if we came here she would help us. Because I knew my mother, I didn't believe what Portia was saying. She was hiding something. But why?

"Why would I fire Beulah? She's an excellent cook, keeps the house clean and puts up with your bullshit. I'd say the only smart thing you've ever done in your life was hire her. I thought for a moment there you possessed some compassion I had missed when she told me how you helped her and Heidi. I see I'm wrong. That's disappointing."

Jasper dropped his hands to his sides that had been crossed over his chest. "I've got things to do. You can continue your pointless routine of living," he told Portia. Then he turned to me. "I need to speak with you about a business matter. Please meet me in the pool house in thirty minutes."

Then he turned and left the room.

I stood slowly. I wanted to apologize to Portia, but I wasn't sure if I owed her an apology. She was hard to understand. The longer Jasper was around, the colder she became. Instead of trying to smooth things, I said, "I'll get your coffee now."

She didn't respond.

Chapter Fourteen

PORTIA HAD IGNORED me completely when I brought her coffee and a bowl of fresh strawberries. She was angry—with me or Jasper I wasn't sure. Probably both.

I didn't have time to worry about it. Jasper wanted to meet with me about business which I didn't exactly understand. Unless he meant he had more chores for me or he wanted more groceries. Although I couldn't imagine that was the case. I'd stocked his kitchen well in the pool house.

When the time came to meet with Jasper, he was inside the pool house, so I knocked instead of walking inside.

"Come in," he called.

I opened the door to see him on the sectional leather sofa with a computer on his lap, his right ankle resting on his left knee to prop up the computer and a cup of coffee in his hand.

He smiled. "Punctual. Good. Please have a seat."

I walked over and sat on the chair that faced the sofa. There was a large wooden barrel that was once filled with Makers Mark Whiskey according to the black labeling on its side. Now it was a coffee table.

"This morning with Portia went about as smoothly as I had imagined. I know you were hoping for a more definitive answer. But if there is one, I'm afraid we will never know it. That isn't why I asked you to meet me out here, however.

After breakfast, I was out here going through emails and the endless bills, investment, and correspondence with Van Allan Industries that have come through just this week. It's a lot of paper filing I don't have time for. Jed Bankhead has been handling everything since my father's death. My father's personal secretary became Jed's. She was to become mine when I was ready to completely take over next year but two days ago his wife walked in on Jed and Bethany, the secretary, naked on Jed's desk in the Chicago office," he paused and took a drink of coffee. "Gotta love marriage and happily ever after's, huh? Anyway, I can't run Van Allan industries yet. I am still learning; working in the Savannah offices now to learn, which are the smallest of the three and the newest. There will be sexual harassment filed by Bethany I am sure when Jed let's her go. More bullshit that he has to handle. But here in Savannah I need help.

The actual building was serving as a meeting location when personnel from the other officers came into town to meet with my father after he relocated here. After his passing, it hasn't been used much. That's what I've been doing. Moving people here to make it a functioning office. An office so Van Allen Industries can expand into the southern states and have a central location. I need some help with organizing all the piles of paperwork that have been ignored at the office here. I am looking for a qualified administrative assistant, of course, but for now I just need some extra hands. I know you need another job. Working nights isn't going to be enough for you if you want to keep Heidi in the home she's currently in. I'd like you to work in the offices for three hours a day Monday through Friday. You'd continue your duties here of course. I'm willing to pay you fifty dollars an hour which will average about $750 a week. This would help me and fix my current problem as well as help you."

Seven hundred and fifty dollars a week was a lot. It would be more than I needed to take care of Heidi when added to my income from cleaning. If I kept my night job then I could put money away for college. "Are you offering this intending for me to quit my evening job?" I asked.

He frowned. "I'd hoped you would. You looked exhausted this morning. But I'm not demanding you do anything. That's up to you."

"I could cut back my hours there if the manager would be okay with it. If I worked there a couple nights a week then I would be able to save for college."

He nodded. "Fair enough."

It was that easy. He was giving me a way to make more money. He wasn't demanding anything of me. I took a long, easy breath. The first full breath I'd taken in three days. Heidi was going to be fine. And now I'd have a chance to get my nursing degree.

"Thank you, Jasper. Thank you so much."

He grinned. The kind of grin that I was sure made most women lightheaded. It made me feel a little swoony. That was a bad thing though. I couldn't look at Jasper that way. He was my boss. He held the power to break me. His smile, the way he wore a pair of jeans, and his sculpted chest that I still could picture clearly after his never ending pool party were of no consequence to me.

"You can start tomorrow. However, after you're done inside, we can ride over to the office and I can show you everything. Introduce you to the staff there."

"Okay," I said as I stood up. "I should be ready to go in two hours."

"Very well. See you then."

As I hurried out of the pool house, I couldn't get the silly smile off my face. I was going to be okay. We both were. I'd make cupcakes this week. Heidi would never understand we had a reason to celebrate, but that was more than okay.

This Jasper was so different than the one I thought he was when he arrived. He was all business and mature in there. But the party he had held was a much different Jasper. At the party, he was the spoiled trust fund kid with nothing to worry about in life. I liked this Jasper much better. I just couldn't figure out his choice in friends.

The next two hours flew by as I hurried to get everything done, then changed into the only nice dress I owned. My mother had made the pale blue sundress for me three months before she got sick. She'd made it for me to wear to a job interview at the bank. A job I didn't get because I needed Saturdays off to take care of Heidi.

Mom would have been so excited about my new job. She'd love that I wore her dress. The silver flats that were my correct size and that I reserved for special occasions had also been bought by her. I slipped them on and my toes thanked me.

I quickly made my way to the doors leading to the pool house to meet Jasper, passing Portia as she came down the staircase with her white tennis outfit on. Her hair was pulled up neatly in a ponytail. But she was scowling at me.

"Why are you dressed like that?" she snapped.

"I'm going to the office with Jasper. He needs me to organize and file paperwork."

She rolled her eyes. "Sure he does. He's just like his father." She stalked past me and the expensive perfume she wore filled the air.

I wanted to defend myself and tell her that Jasper did, in fact, need me to organize for him. But she was gone. Maybe I should have apologized earlier.

Chapter Fifteen

WHEN JASPER SAID the office was new and small I imagined something much different from the twenty-story building made of glass we were walking into. Van Allan Industries was written on the front door and the sign out front. There was a doorman and a front desk where you check in upon entering.

A young attractive brunette, whose eyes locked on Jasper the moment we entered, smiled brightly. "Good afternoon, Mr. Van Allan."

He paused at her desk. "Brandy Jo, I'd like you to meet Beulah Edwards. She will be coming in for a few hours every day to do some work for me."

Brandy Jo gave me a tight smile. "It's nice to meet you."

"It's nice to meet you, too," I replied with a sincerer smile, hoping I could thaw her iciness.

Her gaze swung right back to Jasper. And her bright smile returned. "Can I get you coffee?"

"That'd be wonderful, Brandy Jo. Thank you. I'll be in my office. Send someone up with it in about twenty minutes."

Brandy Jo blushed. I couldn't help but wonder what else Brandy Jo did for Jasper. He hadn't seemed very upset about Jed having an affair with his secretary. Maybe all Van Allen employees hooked up in the work place.

Frowning at my thoughts, I figured that wasn't fair to assume. Besides Jasper wasn't married and could sleep with whomever he wanted.

When the elevator doors closed behind us, Jasper turned to me. "I slept with her last week. It was late, and we'd been working all day, we had some wine. She got naked and climbed up on my desk with her legs spread. It was a one-time thing."

"Oh," I said wondering if I had said my thoughts out loud.

He gave me a crooked grin. "You're expressive Beulah. I could see where your head was. I thought I'd clear it up for you."

Because my mouth had a mind of its own, I blurted out, "Do your employees often get naked and get on your desk?"

He laughed loudly. "No. But I've only had employees for two weeks. I'll let you know in a couple months."

I nodded as if that were a reasonable response. He laughed harder then. "God you're fun."

The doors opened at the twentieth floor. Jasper's floor was fancy and impressive. There was a large area with sofas, tables, and magazines. A chandelier hung from the ceiling. There were two large wooden doors ahead of us that seemed to hold the rest of this floor of the building behind them. Jasper pulled a card out of his pocket and touched it to the metal box on the door. A light turned green and the door opened.

"I'll get you a key before you leave," he said, holding his up.

We entered a massive room. Shelves lined the walls to the right and left as we walked by. They were filled with books. Then we came to a bar—a well-stocked bar that was to the left, and to the right was a door that stood open and I could see an elaborate bathroom inside. He motioned for me straight ahead. "Go on in. I'll show you my office then we can walk over to the filing area."

We walked through the next door. His office was filled with large, masculine furnishings and smelled of oak and cigars. The entire back wall was windows overlooking Savannah's business district. It didn't seem like Jasper's style at all.

My gaze fell to his desk and I couldn't help but picture Brandy Jo and him going at it right there with the night view of the city behind them.

"As you can see it's a large desk. Plenty of room for a wild fuck," he said behind me, and I jumped, jerking my gaze from the table as my cheeks heated. Jasper was trying to get a reaction from me and it worked because I was caught thinking about his lewd words.

"I, uh . . ." I had nothing to say to that.

"Relax, Beulah. It was just sex. No need to get nervous. Now, this pile of shit you see on my desk is only yesterday's mail and nonsense that needs to be opened and organized. The rest of it is through that door at the back of my office. I have fifteen filing cabinets, and about ten piles of a complete mess that needs attention. When I offered you such a hefty hourly pay it was because this is a headache. You're not going to enjoy it."

I liked organizing. I could do the filing alone and focus on nothing but the work. "I can start now if you want," I told him.

He went over to his desk and picked up the pile of papers, and with a relieved look on his face he brought them to me. "Sounds good to me. Let's get you to the filing room, and if you have any questions try and figure it out. If you can't, then ask. But honestly, I just need it organized. You do what you think will work best."

We walked through a narrow entrance into a square room lined with filing cabinets. There were no windows and it was like a massive walk in closet. In the center of the room was a bigger pile of papers than I had imagined. He wasn't kidding about the mess.

"See, it's not going to be easy," he said, as I looked at the job in front of me.

"I'll get to work on it now."

"Okay then. When you're done for the day I can call a car service to take you home."

"Thanks."

He started to walk out, but paused. "I can pay you in advance this month if you need it."

The concern in his eyes was nice. He cared.

"I don't owe anything for two more weeks," I answered.

"I'll make sure you have your first month pay by then."

"That would be great. Thank you."

He didn't say anything else before he turned and left.

I stood looking down at the most insane scattered mess on the floor and smiled. This would take time. I had plenty to do and this was really going to help Jasper. It wasn't a hand out because he felt sorry for me. It was a job. One he needed organized desperately. That fact made me feel much better about this situation.

The next couple of hours, I got lost in my task. When I glanced down at my watch, I realized I needed to get back to the house to do a few things before I went to my evening job at the club. I enjoyed being tucked away in this room alone with the files. I was dreading working at the club tonight. But if I ever wanted to go to nursing school, I needed to start putting money away.

Standing in front of the desk, I surveyed the pile of papers with a smile of satisfaction. I slipped my shoes back on and walked out into Jasper's office. He was standing with his hands tucked in his pockets, talking on the speaker phone. I paused, hoping he saw me. The call sounded like business with someone in his Chicago office from the brief snippet of conversation I heard.

He turned before I heard too much and gave me a slight nod.

"I have an appointment, John. We'll talk later. Just go ahead and use Samantha for that area," he said, then walked over and ended the call.

"You ready to leave?"

"Yes, please. I need to finish at the house before I leave for work tonight."

Jasper frowned. "This is going to be a long day for you."

"Or productive," I replied.

He grinned then. "That's putting a positive spin on things."

The door to his office opened, grabbing our attention. Stone wasn't dressed like he belonged here. His clothes weren't surprising though because the jeans and T-shirt combo was all I ever saw him in.

Stone's eyes went from Jasper to me, then back to Jasper. "You ready for lunch?"

It was almost three o'clock.

"I forgot. I need to get Beulah home first. Let's take her on our way."

"Why is she here?" Stone asked, sounding more annoyed than anything.

"She's organizing that shit back there for me," Jasper said. "Stop acting like an ass."

Stone didn't look my way again. "Then let's go. I'm starving."

"As always, a charmer." Jasper was clearly amused by his friend's scowl.

I wondered if Jasper was the only friend he had and that was why he was always around. With a personality like that I didn't imagine anyone could like him much.

"How many jobs does she need?" Stone asked finally, flicking his gaze my way but only for a moment.

"Not your business," Jasper told him then winked at me.

"No, but it's your fucking business so I hope you're thinking clearly." The way he said it made it sound like I was somehow using Jasper. It was insulting.

"I can handle some things on my own, Stone." This time he didn't sound as amused.

I wondered about his choice of words though. "Some things" was an odd way of explaining our situation. What was it he couldn't handle on his own?

"Sure, let's get going so I can eat."

I wanted to point out he didn't do anything all day and could eat whenever he wanted, but I kept my mouth shut.

Jasper started talking about a party he wanted to have next weekend for Tate's birthday At least that kept them busy and their top of conversation off me until I was dropped at home.

I would make sure that I wasn't scheduled to work Saturday night at the club. I had a party to serve it would seem.

Chapter Sixteen

THE FIRST THING I saw when I walked into the employees only room at the club was the back of Shauna's red head as she knelt in front of Neil who was holding the back of her head as he groaned with pleasure. I stopped dead in my tracks. They didn't seem to notice me. Neil's eyes were closed and his other hand was on the wall for support I assumed.

"Fuck, Shauna, fuck that's good, baby," he said just as his eyes opened to look down at her, but he caught sight of me and locked his sex-hungered gaze on me instead. I expected him to stop her or . . . something. I didn't expect a slow smile to appear on his face as he continued to let her go at it.

"I'm gonna come," he said as he kept looking at me.

My face heated. I wanted to run from the room but my feet seemed to be cemented to the floor. I was in shock.

"Uh," he said his eyes slightly closing. "Ohhyeah! Oh, fuck. Here it comes," he said leaning heavily on the wall now as he let out a long low groan of satisfaction.

I spun around and ran from the room.

I hadn't been prepared to witness that. I wish I'd been able to move sooner. Run faster. Jeez! They didn't even lock the door.

"Going the wrong way, aren't you?" Carey said as he stepped out of his office. "You need to get dressed in your uniform first."

I opened my mouth to say something when Shauna spoke. "Show's over. You can use the room to get dressed now."

I couldn't look at her.

Carey chuckled like he knew exactly what had just happened. "Breaking in the new girl early, I see."

I needed to talk to Carey about my hours, but at this moment, I just wanted to find a closet or quiet space to compose myself. My pink cheeks made me look like an innocent school girl—the entire staff would make fun of me now.

I didn't wait around for more laughter and comments. I hurried back to the room forgetting that Neil hadn't exited yet. However, when I came face to face with him as I opened the door, I remembered. Dang it.

Neil's lips curled up at the edges. "Sorry about that."

He didn't look sorry at all.

"There's a lock on the door," I pointed out.

"Yeah," he agreed. "But what's the fun in locking it? Takes away from the thrill of someone walking in and watching."

I didn't say anything to that crude comment. I started to step around him when his hand touched my arm. "I'm sorry. I'd say that was a moment of lust and I needed some relief, but honestly, you'll need to adjust to seeing things like that around here. It's kind of an open thing with the others." He paused as if he were thinking about his next words. "And Shauna gives one hell of a blow job."

"I'll keep that in mind," I said tugging my arm free as I hurried past him inside.

"You'll warm up to it. And I look forward to when you do," he said and left the room.

I let out a sigh of relief as he shut the door, and I allowed myself a second to compose myself. Changing in here now seemed more vulnerable than before. I didn't want someone walking in when I was alone, thinking I was interested in . . . something else. I'd come to work dressed from now on. If the employees and owner wanted to share all the STD's they were likely to get screwing around like they were, I didn't have to be a part of it.

Getting through this first official night and finding time to talk to Carey about my work hours was all I should have been focused on. Unfortunately, it got busy early and I never found the chance to talk to him.

At the end of my shift, I counted my money, and I did get over one hundred dollars in tips. Monday must be a good night at the club, and now I felt like it was worth the lack of sleep I'd be feeling tomorrow.

Neil and a blonde waitress flirted most of the evening. He even gave me a suggestive grin more than once. That guy had serious issues. I'd decided he was a manwhore, until his wife came in for a drink after her work shift ended. Then I realized he was a manwhore adulterer. *Yuck.*

When I finally walked into the house at three in the morning, I found Stone sitting in the great room with the gas fire going, even though it was only sixty degrees outside. He looked up from the book in his lap and didn't smile. Not that I expected him to. He never smiled.

"Why are you working three jobs?" he asked.

I was too tired for this. For him. "Why are you sitting in Jasper's house at three in the morning drinking his whiskey?"

His only change of expression was an almost unnoticeable quirk of his brow as he said, "Because he has a stripper he brought home from the club in the pool house. She's currently calling him 'God' and begging him to fuck her up the ass harder. Now answer my question."

I was sleepy. No, I was exhausted, but his words woke me up. Jasper brought a stripper home?

"Uh," I started to explain. A second later, I forgot what I was going to say. I looked up to find Stone's quirky brow had turned into a cold glare, and that snapped me out of my lost thoughts. "I need money. I'm saving it for nursing school. Any more questions? I'm tired."

He studied me a moment, then returned his focus to his book. "No."

I continued walking through the room and his voice stopped me just before I walked out. "I didn't expect you to have ambition or goals."

Maybe it was the lack of sleep, or maybe I had just met my quota with Stone's crap that caused my next words to spew out unfiltered. "Of course you didn't. You're too busy glaring at me down that long nose of yours."

Then I fled, because I had been rude and the words I'd said were partially untrue. First of all, Stone had a nice nose. It wasn't long at all. And second, I had just snapped at my boss's friend. To add to my mortification, I had a sneaking suspicion Stone was Jasper's best friend because he never left the house.

I didn't stop until I was in my room in the basement.

I undressed quickly, and after a quick shower, I collapsed in bed. I decided I would worry about apologizing to Stone tomorrow.

Unfortunately, when I closed my eyes, my mind wandered back to Stone's words. I saw Jasper and some unknown stripper doing things I'd never done. And deep down I had to admit I didn't like that Jasper was with someone else. That wasn't a good thing. I had to suppress my unwanted jealousy because being attracted to my boss was not okay. I needed my job here and at the office desperately. Jasper was going to sleep with a lot of women and I needed to get right with watching them come and go. Still, I had to admit I was a little disappointed in him. The guy I was getting to know was somewhat likable.

I tried hard to push his face out of my head and thoughts. It wasn't possible.

When I finally fell asleep, I dreamed of him.

That was the beginning.

Chapter Seventeen

M Y DREAMS HAD been vivid last night. So much so that when I walked into the kitchen with pancakes and sausage for Jasper, I blushed. I'd wondered if he'd bring the girl with him to breakfast, but he hadn't. He was alone.

"This smells amazing," he said to me as I sat his plate in front of him. His phone was in his hand and he was texting, but he stopped to look at me.

"Thanks," I said. My cheeks still felt warm. I quickly turned away hoping he wouldn't notice.

"You okay this morning?" he asked me before I could leave the room.

"Yes."

"Late night at work?"

"Yes."

He chuckled. "Okay. Well, I won't keep you."

I nodded and hurried out. I felt silly. I looked silly. When I got to the kitchen, I sighed in frustration as I leaned against the bar. This wasn't going to work. I had to get over last night's dream, and over my attraction to Jasper. He was helping me. I didn't receive help from many people, especially not from someone who looked like him. I had to keep my feelings straight. I was grateful to him for my job here and for the additional work he'd offered me at his office. That did not mean I was attracted to him.

I rolled my eyes at myself. I sounded ridiculous. A day experiencing Jasper's charm, and then my erotic dream probably inspired by what I'd witnessed at work had me all a mess.

Jasper cleared his throat behind me, causing me to jump before I spun around.

"I was wondering if you'd like to have breakfast with me. It's lonely in there." He was carrying his plate in one hand and his coffee in the other. He sat both down on the bar.

Bad idea. "Where's Stone?" I asked.

"Gone already. He went running before going into the office."

Office? "Stone works?"

Jasper nodded. "Yeah. He does. For me. Now, why don't you eat the food you made for him and let me enjoy your company. Please," he added.

The way he tilted his head and his eyes reflected the morning sunlight coming in the windows made it hard to say no.

I nodded and joined him. Even though he'd spent last night with a stripper, I liked him. I could never do more than like him. It was bad for me to like him.

I was going to work on that.

"Okay. Can I get you more coffee?"

"No. I just require your company."

He just requires my company. *Ugh. That damn dream.*

I went to the cabinet, pulled out a plate and put half of the portion I'd made for Stone on the plate. Jasper watched me and feeling his gaze on me made me nervous.

"What time did you get in last night?" he asked.

"Three," I told him as I put my plate down beside him and took a seat on the stool.

"I hope you're taking tonight off. That's two nights in a row. You need rest."

I'd never spoken to Carey last night. "I didn't get a chance to talk to the manager last night."

"Call him, Beulah."

I could call him. That made sense. "Okay. I'll probably have to because it's busy when I get there at night making it hard to find time to talk to him about it."

He didn't say much the next few minutes as he ate and drank his coffee. I took that time to plan what I'd say to Carey over the phone.

"Portia left last night. Said she was going to stay with a friend of hers in the Hamptons for the rest of the summer. You won't have as much work to do in the house now. If you can get in more hours at the office that's okay with me."

I stopped with my fork midway to my mouth. *Portia was gone?* "She left?"

"We don't exactly get along," he said.

"That's why she left?"

He shrugged. "Don't know. Don't care. Less bullshit for me to deal with."

Would he leave too? How long would the filing job last and then what? What if my being here was no longer needed?

"I want you to stay here. Hell, I need you to stay here. I don't have time to find someone dependable and trustworthy to live in this house and take care of it."

He was reading my mind again.

I nodded. "You're good at that," I finally said.

"I'm good at a lot of things. You need to be more specific." His tone was teasing but I wondered what things he was referring to.

"Knowing what I'm thinking."

"You've got very expressive eyes."

I'd never been told that before. Guys had complimented me, telling me my eyes were beautiful but never that they were expressive. Maybe he just paid closer attention.

He was being kind again. Making it hard to remember I shouldn't lean close to smell his cologne, or study the way his smiles were all different, or admire the way he looked in his clothing. If he caught me doing those things, I was sure to be kicked out after he fired me from both my jobs.

I took one last bite and stood up. Making myself indispensable around here was the way to make sure the jobs didn't end. Crushing on Jasper was not. "I'll get to work upstairs and then I'll be at the office by eleven, if that is okay."

"Yeah. That's good."

"I'll make sure to do a deep cleaning in the pool house this morning too."

He didn't respond immediately.

He finally said, "Yeah, that's good. I'll be moving into my room upstairs today. While Stone is here working for me, he'll stay in the pool house. You don't have to stock the kitchen for him though."

"Okay, I'll make sure your room and bathroom are ready for you then."

He smirked. "Why are you so nervous today, Beulah?"

That was the million dollar question wasn't it? One he was not ever getting the answer to.

I shrugged to buy time to answer him. "I'm not. I just need more coffee to get fully awake."

He didn't look like he believed me. He kept smirking. "I like it. I think it's cute."

Why, oh why, was he doing this? It was embarrassing enough. I kept my eyes averted from his view so he couldn't magically read my thoughts and see last night's dream in them.

I heard his stool push across the tile floor as he stood, and I knew he was getting ready to leave. Thank God.

"I'll see you at work," he said.

"Yeah, see you then," I replied but didn't turn around. I lifted a hand as if to wave which was stupid. It seemed all I could manage to do today was stupid stuff.

Chapter Eighteen

FINDING SOMETHING TO wear to the office a second day wasn't easy. I decided on a pair of white shorts that were nicer than my other shorts and a black top. My flats and a necklace helped dress it up a bit. I didn't know if it mattered what I wore. I was in a back room alone with paperwork. I put some effort into how I looked anyway.

Brandy Jo wasn't all smiles for me when I walked in—not the way she was for Jasper—but I greeted her with a friendly smile anyway. Her response was a cold stare. I wasn't her competition, the world was. She needed to understand how Jasper worked. I almost felt sorry for her.

The card that Jasper had given me to enter the protected area of the building was tucked in my purse. I reached for it and slipped it out while the elevator took me to his floor. My job with Van Allen Industries was only filing papers but it felt important. Like I had fancy responsibilities in a position that you could only get with a degree. I didn't want to work in an office like this forever. Being a nurse had been my dream since I was a little girl. For now, I would enjoy this experience and I was thankful to Jasper for giving it to me.

When the elevators opened, I walked into the waiting area that was beautiful and just as empty as it had been yesterday. I doubted many people actually waited in this area. Which was a shame. It was such a nice place to wait.

The door clicked as it unlocked easily with a wave of my key card. I knocked lightly before pushing it open in case Jasper was busy. There was no response, so I went in. His office was empty as I made my way to the back room where I filed.

For the next hour, I opened envelopes and made piles according to the subject matter all around me.

The smell of food caught my attention and I looked up from my work just as Jasper walked into the filing room holding two paper bags.

His eyebrows were raised as he looked at me among my piles and said, "I brought lunch. Come in here and help me eat it."

It smelled incredible and my stomach growled reminding me I hadn't eaten since early that morning.

Standing, I straightened my shorts and slipped my shoes back on. "Thank you. I was getting hungry. I didn't think about packing a lunch."

"Then that works out good for me. I need a lunch date and I bought all this food."

I wanted to think he'd bought it for me to eat with him, but I knew better. It was very likely he had bought it with other plans that had fallen through.

"How are the pits of hell coming along in there?" he asked me as we stepped into his office and he placed the bags on his desk.

"It's not that bad," I told him. "I enjoy it. The organizing. Makes me feel like I'm accomplishing something."

He gave me a crooked grin that I tried not to stare at. "Not sure what that says about you, Beulah." He was teasing. I could tell, so I just smiled in response.

The door to his office opened before he finished unloading the bags. It was Stone. *Oh joy. Perfect way to ruin lunch.*

"You eating in here?" he asked. Again, he was dressed like he was going to a frat party, not to work with Jasper.

"Yes, and there isn't enough for three. I thought you had a business lunch."

He shrugged. "It's over. Not hungry," he paused and glanced briefly at me. "Just didn't expect you to be eating in here." He left out the "with her", but it was understood in the tone of his voice.

"Better company in here," Jasper told him, and at that moment, I wanted to kiss Jasper's face. He had no problem with me. He didn't think I was below him. Sure, I worked for him but he accepted me as a human. Unlike Stone.

"I've got the contract I picked up at lunch today if you want to go over it while you eat."

I didn't look at either of them. I kept my eyes focused on the food Jasper was placing in front of me. I felt like I was in the way, like most of the time Stone was around. He managed to make me feel awkward and unwanted.

"I'm going to enjoy my lunch date, and then I'll look it over. Leave it on the desk."

Again, the urge to kiss Jasper emerged.

"Date?" Stone asked, his voice sounding displeased as if the word "date" was crude or distasteful.

"Yes, Stone. Date."

"She's your employee," Stone told him as if he'd somehow forgotten.

"Jesus, you can be an ass," Jasper said with a chuckle. "Can you leave us to our lunch if all you're going to do is be a dick?"

My phone that never ever rang began to ring. I didn't have an unlimited calling plan. It was a prepaid phone I kept for emergencies only, or in case Heidi needed me. My heart was already pounding when I quickly jerked it out of my pocket and said, "Hello."

"Hello, may I speak with Beulah," the lady on the other end of the line said.

"Yes, this is Beulah."

"This is Stacy McDavid from Among the Spanish Moss group home and I'm calling because Heidi isn't well. The doctor just came to see her, and she has the flu. She won't eat, and she's crying for you."

Heidi getting sick was never a good thing. Little things could be harder on her than others. "She had her flu shot. How did she get the flu?" I asked already walking back to the room where I had left my purse. I had to see her.

"It still happens. There are many strains of the flu. The doctor is going to monitor her, and if he feels she needs to be hospitalized he will."

Hospital? Oh, God. I had to get there. Abruptly, I felt sick.

"I'm on my way. Tell her I'm on my way."

"I will."

I ended the call and grabbed my purse, then ran from the room back into the office.

"Heidi is sick. I need to leave."

Jasper was already standing up, his food forgotten. He grabbed a set of keys off his desk. "I'll take you."

He'll take me? "Why?"

He came around the table, and his hand reached for and was now touching my elbow. "Let's go. You don't need to drive upset and you need a friend right now. Think of me as support."

"What about the meeting in an hour?" Stone asked.

"Cancel it," was Jasper's response as he led me out of the office.

"You don't have to do this. It's very kind of you but I can get there. I will be fine."

He shook his head. "No. You're a mess. I can feel you trembling. I'm going with you. Besides, it's time I met Heidi."

Jasper was beautiful. He was kind. He had helped me when I needed someone. All those things had led to the dream I'd had of him. I knew that. But this . . . this act . . . My heart melted and I knew I was in trouble. As hard as I fought it, I knew I was falling in love with him and that was the biggest mistake I could make. But I had no idea how to stop it. Jasper wasn't the kind of guy you loved.

My heart didn't seem to get that memo though. It was falling anyway.

Chapter Nineteen

WHEN WE WALKED in the doors at Heidi's home, I didn't stop at the front desk like I normally did. I hurried down the wing of the right hall with Jasper following right behind me.

Heidi still had a private room and all of the private rooms were on the first floor, right wing. One of the reasons I was happy she had that room was it was closer to the activities. She was so social and being stuck on another floor away from everything seemed sad to me.

Her door had a bright yellow sunflower she had made in the activity room from ribbons and burlap hanging on it. When she'd shown it to me last week, she had been so proud of it. They made new door decorations each month here and she always looked forward to what they would make next. I wondered if she had to share her door with her roommate when they moved her to another room. That was a silly thing to worry about right now but I did anyway.

Stopping at her door, I looked up at Jasper. He'd driven here, parked, helped calm me down by listening to what was wrong with her and reassured me that the flu was common. He was sure she'd be okay. This was a good facility and they'd take care of her. All those things were true and I had needed reminding.

Heidi hadn't been sick since Momma had passed away. This was the first time I would face Heidi being ill without Momma. I'd felt terrified and alone when they called me, and then Jasper had stepped in.

"Thank you," I said. Those two words weren't enough for all he'd just done for me. He had no idea how him being there helped.

"You're welcome," he said and a small smile touched his too handsome for words face.

"You shouldn't come in here. You could get the flu," I pointed out.

His smile turned into a smirk. "I like to live dangerously. Let's go."

I didn't argue. With a nod, I opened the door and went inside.

Heidi's pale face asleep on the two pillows she required gripped my heart. She looked small right now. I hurried to her side and held her hand with mine. She was warm, but she'd have a fever with the flu.

I thought of all the things Momma did for us when we were sick as kids. What was it Heidi liked best?

"She'll be full of questions when she wakes up and sees you. Be prepared for anything."

"I look forward to it. Why don't you sit down and relax? You've been a ball of nerves since you got the call. Sit here and watch her sleep. I'll go find you coffee and something to eat. You've got to be starving by now."

We never ate our lunch. "Don't worry about me. Get something for yourself. There are some nice places near here."

He frowned. "I'm not leaving you to get myself something to eat. I'll get us both some terrible coffee and a candy bar if that's all I can find in this place."

"Okay . . . but that's an accurate guess. There is a vending machine room to your right and one length of the hall down. They have terrible coffee and candy bars. I think they have some crackers too, if you want to go that route."

"I may get crazy and get both," he said teasingly before he stepped out of the room and left me there.

He could have left here. Gone and enjoyed his lunch. Anyone else would have. But he was staying to eat snack foods and drink bad coffee with me. My heart squeezed again and my eyes suddenly felt damp. I'd never had that. Of course, Momma had always been there. But as far as someone to care and understand about Heidi, there hadn't ever been anyone else.

Guys had asked me out in high school. I'd dated a few for months at a time, but they never wanted to come to my house. They avoided getting to know my family. It was as if they wanted to pretend that my family didn't exist. That I didn't live in a trailer on the bad side of town and my sister didn't have Down syndrome.

When Heidi started attending school with me I'd pass her classroom and stop to visit her and her classmates. She was always so excited to see me and introduced me over and over again. Not once had any guy I'd dated gone with me to her room. They always made a quick escape. Having Jasper here was nice. Being able to share the most important part of my life with him meant something. And it shouldn't. I knew I was going to get hurt and he wouldn't even mean to.

Heidi's eyes slowly fluttered open and she smiled as she focused on me. I squeezed her hand in mine. "Hello, sleeping beauty."

"Beulah," she said in a groggy voice. "You came cause I'm sick."

I didn't want her to be scared. "Yes. But you're going to get all better. The doctor has medicine for you."

"I want Momma," she said her smile falling.

I wanted Momma too. Every day that passed I missed her. This was the first time in months Heidi had asked for her.

"I know. If she was here she'd be right by your side. Singing the songs you love in her pretty voice."

"Why is she in Heaven?"

I had answered this question many times too. I wanted to tell her I didn't know and it was unfair. That God knew we needed her and he shouldn't have taken her, but that wasn't what Heidi needed to hear. That was for me to be angry about.

"Because God thought she'd make a beautiful angel." That had been my story all along. The one I knew Heidi would love. The one that would make her smile. And just like always, she smiled.

"She's the prettiest angel in Heaven now."

"Yes, she is," I agreed. "And right now, she is watching you, and making sure the doctors take care of you. I bet if you close your eyes and listen closely, you can hear her singing."

Heidi's eyes lit up and she looked around the room as if Momma might suddenly appear. How I wish that could happen. "Really?" she asked. Her voice was full of wonder.

"Oh, yes. I close my eyes at night and I listen for her until I fall asleep. Sometimes, right before I doze off, I hear her pretty voice."

Heidi was listening so intently she didn't notice the door

opening, but I heard it. I knew Jasper was back and her questions would begin. I glanced back at him and he was carrying two vending machine coffees and his pockets were stuffed with junk food. "I brought a friend," I told Heidi. "He wanted to meet you so he came with me."

"Jasper, this is my favorite person in the world who also happens to be my sister, Heidi. Heidi, this is my friend Jasper." I didn't explain to her he was my boss. That was more than she could figure out at one time. Calling him my friend would make more sense to her.

"Hello, Heidi. It's nice to finally meet you. Your sister talks about you all the time," Jasper said as he handed me a cup of coffee.

"You're handsome like a movie star," Heidi said, and then blushed. Her already warm cheeks turned an even deeper red.

"Thank you. You're a beauty just like your sister."

"Are you going to marry her?" Heidi asked, her eyes wide with wonder.

This was what I expected. Heidi had the idea that all couples got married. The friendship thing didn't really register to her. Just last week she told me she was going to marry Jimmy, a guy she liked here. Two weeks before she was going to marry Brent.

"Jasper is my friend. Remember how we talked about having friends?" I asked in an attempt to remind her. She was very hung up on the boyfriend thing.

"He looks like a movie star. You should marry him," she argued.

I laughed then. "Yes, he does, but that doesn't mean I should marry him."

She frowned. "I don't see why not."

I leaned back in my chair and took a sip of my coffee. Glancing up at Jasper, I saw him grinning and I was relieved he wasn't panicking. "If I wanted to get married—which I never do, but if I did—I'd definitely be interested in your sister," Jasper told her.

"You don't want to get married? Why? You could have babies and play games and eat ice cream."

He didn't laugh at that and I had to give him credit. "Those are very true points. But I'm too busy with work. I don't have time for all the fun things that come with marriage."

"Do you work on the movies?"

This time I had to bite back my laugher. Heidi was staring up at him completely focused. her flu forgotten.

"I'm afraid not. I work at a very boring job in an office most of the day."

She seemed displeased by that. "You should go work on Days of Our Lives. It's my favorite Soap, and the nurses here too. We watch it every day at lunch time. You would be the most hand-somest man on the movie."

Jasper grinned. "I'll keep that in mind. If this office thing doesn't work out, that will be my backup."

She seemed appeased by that and began telling him all about yesterday's episode. He took a seat beside me and handed me a pack of peanut butter crackers, chocolate donuts and a crispy wafer bar. I reached for the crackers, ripped open the package, and began to eat them.

Heidi talked to Jasper who kept up the conversation. It went from soap operas, to her love for Jimmy, to her best friend May, to pizza day being her favorite day. He seemed happy to talk to her. He even managed to eat the sleeve of bite-sized donuts and the wafer bar while he answered her questions and asked his own.

With each passing minute, I fell more for this man, knowing

it could never lead to anything. He was nothing like I'd first assumed. He was going to be a good friend. That much I knew. I'd
do anything for him after today.

He spent time with me and my sister, and then sat beside me
while the nurse came in to check her vitals.

When visiting hours were up, I kissed Heidi's forehead and
told her I loved her. She told me she loved me too, and that she
was going to listen for Momma's singing tonight. Then she told
Jasper to come see her again.

I didn't know if he would but I knew she'd remember him
after this day. And so would the nurses. On our way out, every
eye followed him and I was brought back to the reality that he
would never belong to me. He had been perfect with Heidi. And
I loved him—I knew that now. It was impossible not to.

But he was my boss and would be until my job was done.
Then I'd move on in life. The idea made me sad.

Chapter Twenty

JASPER

THE QUIET, EARLY morning was peaceful. I stood with a cup of coffee I had made for myself and watched the pool ripple with the breeze. It was skimmed and clean right now. That would end though. The party would start in the late afternoon and would last most of the night. Girls would be topless, drinks would be in abundance, and the people I called my friends would surround me.

The parties helped me get by. To forget the bad shit. To remember that this was my life. The one I had been born into. The one my father had left for me. But he had messed up the plans. I had never expected to take over Van Allen Industries this soon. I had plans to travel and enjoy life after graduation, not deal with employees and my mother. Coming back here had been the last thing I had wanted to do.

Now, I was here and I was doing exactly what I'd planned when I'd faced the fact I had to return. If I didn't, my mother would ruin me. Nothing had been the way I thought it would be. Stone had agreed to stay to be my support system. He had his own shit to handle, but he knew I needed help facing Portia and this company. He was levelheaded where I . . . wasn't. I was the dreamer. The one who lost sight of goals to chase new ones.

Glancing back at the house, I wondered if Beulah was awake yet. Just thinking about her made me smile. That wasn't okay and I knew it. She was smart and as I was learning, pretty savvy. She had more shit to deal with than I did. I still couldn't figure out why my mother had helped her and Heidi, but I was glad she had. Beulah had become my reason to smile when I got up every morning. That was fucked up and I knew it.

She made my mornings so much better. The past couple of days she'd eaten breakfast with me. We had talked. My going to see Heidi had thawed her where I was concerned and I got to see the real Beulah. She laughed loudly at my jokes. She blushed if I ever complimented her, and now she was relaxed around me.

The problem with all that was I wanted to grab her and kiss her. Touch her. See if she was as sweet tasting as she'd seemed. Damn sweet little thing was messing with my head. I didn't do relationships of any kind. Ever. And Beulah didn't do quick, no strings attached fucks. I knew that without asking. She was the kind of girl I never messed with. And still, she'd made her way into my thoughts. She'd become my reason for smiling. And I was fighting it every step of the way.

This party was mostly due to my need to fight this attraction. To keep her at arm's length. Because she was getting closer every day, and I was letting it happen. I was bringing her coffee at work just to sit and talk to her. I was canceling meetings just for an excuse to eat lunch with her. And I'd taken all those damn files and dumped them on the floor in a huge clusterfuck just to have a reason to give her the money she needed to take care of Heidi. I knew her pride wasn't going to let me pay her what Portia had been paying her after I overreacted and behaved like a dick.

I ran my hand through my hair and sighed. I was sinking and I had to claw my way out. Tonight, I'd enjoy naked women who plastered themselves to me. I'd probably sleep with a couple at the same time. I would do whatever I needed to get that sweet fucking face out of my head. And God, her smell. I had to forget how good she smelled. Like motherfucking sunshine and honey. Jesus, that was getting to me too.

"Good morning," her voice was soft and almost musical as it floated through the morning breeze. I turned to see her standing just outside the door. A cup of coffee in her hands. For me. "I'm sorry you had to make your own cup."

"I was up earlier than normal. I can manage. You drink that one."

She took a sip then gave me that smile that did things to my chest and my fucking dick. When she stepped back to walk inside, the smart thing to do would have been to just let her go. But I didn't do that.

"Come have coffee with me. It's early. Portia is gone. No need for you to start working yet."

That smile beamed brighter. If Stone came out here, he was going to be a bastard to both of us. And he should be. I had asked him to keep me in check with her. He had no problem ignoring women. When he wanted one, he took her. When he was done, he walked away. The dude was coldhearted and brutal. He was disgusted with my weakness where Beulah was concerned. He had also sensed it from day one. He'd warned me to keep a distance.

I'd tried, but the more I'd tried, the more I wanted to know her.

"Are you enjoying the view before all your friends arrive?" she asked me.

I nodded. "That's exactly what I'm doing."

"Then why have the party? Is it because Stone wants it? "

Stone hated these parties. He wasn't one to be around crowds. He also knew why I needed them. He was behind anything that would keep me at a distance from Beulah.

"I like them. I drink, relax, and enjoy the company."

She didn't respond to that. This would be a good time to start talking about what all she needed to do tonight. What I expected of her. What she needed to be prepared for. That would put her back on her side of the line I had eased her over. The invisible line that was keeping her from being in my arms right now. The line where I remembered she was a girl who was working to take care of her sister and go to nursing school. Not end up naked in my bed then feeling awkward around me until I have to let her go.

I shook my head to clear my thoughts. She needed me. I wasn't going to let my desire for her screw things up. She needed the money, and after witnessing her with her sister I knew I'd do whatever was necessary to protect her. Which meant I wasn't going to touch her.

"Will the caterers be the same?" she asked and I saw her expression was serious. She was already working. Figuring out tonight before I could even start telling her what to do. She was the best kind of employee.

"Yes. Did you like them?" I don't know why I asked her that. Did it matter?

She nodded. "Oh, yes. They're excellent. I just wanted to know what to expect."

"Expect the same as last time. Pretty much the same crowd. You handled yourself well then. Just do the same thing."

She straightened her shoulders and looked determined. The relaxed Beulah who had walked out here to enjoy coffee with me was gone. That was my fault of course. I had steered us in this direction.

"I need to take inventory of the bar—make sure the alcohol order is sufficient. I'll have breakfast ready in an hour. Is that good? Or do you want it sooner?"

All work. Like she should be. This would be what saved us both.

"That will be fine. And Stone will be with me."

I wasn't sure if he would be but I said it anyway as another hurdle to push her back from that line I had been easing her over.

She gave me a tight smile that didn't meet her eyes and went back inside. Her back was straight and her stride would have been determined but she seemed to be limping slightly. I'd ask about that later. Not right now. She needed some space and so did I, because all I wanted to do was go after her and make her laugh, smell her hair, and feel how her body would mold against mine.

Fuck. I needed that alcohol now.

Chapter Twenty-One
BEULAH

PEOPLE WERE FILLING the back yard before five in the evening. I'd been working with the caterer since two-thirty, preparing the poolside and stocking the bar. The caterer wasn't ready for the crowd last time. Monique, the owner, said she had things under control for tonight. I was sure Jasper was paying extra for that.

Jerry, the bartender, was taking college classes here in Savannah. It was his junior year, and this was his extra job. He also worked on a construction crew that was building the new condos in town. He'd left his home over five hundred miles away in south Alabama to attend college here on a partial scholarship. He needed the cash to pay for his books, lodging and food, but his tuition, was paid.

He was a business major. His goal was to open his own restaurant and eventually have a chain of them throughout the southeast. I knew all this because Jerry was also chatty. I didn't mind. We had to do a lot of prep work outside in the bar area. It was nice to talk while we worked. Jerry was also six-foot-three and had a runner's build. Stood to reason his scholarship was for track. His almost black hair and olive complexion was striking set against his crystal blue eyes.

Jerry also informed me he was single. I told him that he'd enjoy tonight because most of the females here would be topless by nine o'clock and they all looked like models.

Jasper had a very elite group of friends. I thought all of his friends looked as if they had just stepped out of a magazine. It was intimidating and overwhelming.

"Take these out to the monsters," Monique said as she handed me a tray of food I didn't recognize. "You don't have to walk around with them. Jasper said that was unnecessary. Just place them over by the bar on the table I set up. We will keep food fresh in that area all night."

I nodded, I already knew this. She'd told me the plan several times. I let her keep telling me because either she was worried about my memory or she was forgetting herself. I didn't look for Jasper or make eye contact with any of the people as I walked to the food area. Seeing Jasper with whatever female he was with tonight wasn't appealing. I didn't want to subject myself to that, which made me pathetic. But at least no one was aware of my feelings for him. I could suffer and save my pride at the same time.

"Beulah," Jerry called after I sat the food down. I walked over to him because the music was too loud to hear from any distance.

"You need something?" I asked him.

"Could you tell Monique that the ice is already melting. We need a cooler out here."

"I'll get you one."

"Thanks."

Jerry was pleasant to work with. If Jasper was going to have these parties often I hoped he used Monique. The three ladies cooking in the kitchen with her inside didn't speak much English, but they were nice. When I asked if it was feta cheese or blue cheese crumbled over a vegetable on a piece of toasted bread because a girl outside had asked me, all three of them just nodded and smiled. I realized then that only Monique could answer questions about the food.

"Why are you limping?" Monique asked as I walked back into the kitchen. "Did you hurt yourself or is that an affliction I didn't notice last time."

The shoes were taking their toll. My toes were bruised, and it was harder to walk without limping. I needed to use some of my next paycheck to buy shoes that fit. I'd been putting it off thinking I could just deal with it, but as soon as I had Heidi's month paid for, I'd shop for new shoes.

"It's the shoes. I'm getting new ones soon. I'll try not to limp."

Monique frowned and looked down at the tennis shoes I was wearing. "They're not heels, darling. Why would tennis shoes make you limp? They don't look new enough to give you blisters."

I needed to get Jerry that cooler and I didn't want to talk about it. "Just uncomfortable," I replied. "Jerry needs a cooler for the ice. Do you have one in the van outside?"

She was still frowning at me. My answer hadn't been sufficient. "Yeah. I meant to grab it. Go ahead and take that next tray of food out, and I'll get the cooler," she said glancing down at my feet one more time before walking away.

I picked up the tray of what I recognized as calamari and headed for the door. One of the ladies called out something to me in Spanish, and I stopped to find out what she wanted. She was running after me with slices of lemon, and placed them around the calamari on the tray as she continued to speak in a language I wished I understood. Then she smiled at me, and gave me a nod and a wave of her hand that it was okay for me to go now.

When I stepped back outside this time, I was careful not to limp or wince. Which I wanted to do both. I thought about putting on my flats that fit me, but they wouldn't work coming in and out of the house carrying food. I could slip and fall. They had no traction and the area around the pool was wet from all the splashing.

I dropped off the tray, then stopped to let Jerry know a cooler was on its way.

"Monique is getting the cooler," I told him as he was shaking a cocktail.

"Great. Thanks," he said as he handed me a can of cherries. "Could you open those and put them in that bowl over there that only has one left."

"Sure." I did as I was told, and just when I was about to toss the empty jar I heard a female squeal Jasper's name. I looked up, I didn't mean to. It was an impulse.

Jasper was carrying a gorgeous blonde around the pool that he had tossed over his shoulder. He had a hand on her bottom that was bare due to the thong she was wearing. She was enjoying it while she slapped at his back. My chest ached. If I could make it not feel anything that would make life so much easier.

"You're so much more appealing than her," Jerry said snapping me out of my thoughts. I had been caught staring.

"Do you need anything else?" I asked him not wanting to focus on what he'd just seen.

Jerry smiled then. He had a dimple in his left cheek. "Guys like that aren't good enough for someone like you. He'd never treat you the way you deserve. I've been around you for a couple hours, and I have spent ninety percent of that time trying to figure out how to ask you on a date or if you were already taken. That guy sees you all the time and he doesn't notice you. And that's because he only sees himself. It's how they are."

I opened my mouth to say something. Although I wasn't sure what.

"That's beautiful. Now Romeo, if you could get me a Maker's Mark that'd be great," Stone's annoyed voice stopped me from having to say anything at all.

"Sure thing," Jerry said with his easy smile. He'd just bashed Jasper and the rest of them, but he was smiling at Stone like he'd said nothing wrong.

"Don't you have a job to do?" Stone asked me. His tone condescending as usual.

I wanted to point out that he wasn't my boss. He worked for Jasper just like I did. But I kept my mouth shut and gave him a short quick nod. With my head held high, I walked away.

I didn't look at Jasper. I didn't look at anyone. I focused on my job.

Chapter Twenty-Two
JASPER

I PUT SASHA down and watched as Stone said something to the bartender and Beulah. She looked upset. I wasn't sure what he'd said but he had been rude. That much I could bet on.

I had barely looked her way all night. There was no reason for him to be a jackass. Annoyed, I walked over to Stone just as he was getting his whiskey. "What did you say?" I asked him, glancing back at the house where Beulah had walked inside.

"I didn't say anything to her. Jesus. I was ordering a fucking whiskey. God knows I need one to deal with this shit. Bunch of elitist shits."

He always acted like he wasn't from the same crowd. From the same home life. He was just like us, only he was angry about it. "I saw you. She walked off looking like she'd been slapped. Lay off all right? She isn't doing anything to deserve that."

Stone smirked then, and turned his eyes toward the bartender who I realized was listening to us as he made a martini. "She might be working, but she's flirting too. I just heard this guy ask her out."

What? I noticed the guy then. He had my complete attention. "You asked her out? She works three jobs. She can't go out." As I said the words, I felt like a jerk.

His eyebrows shot up. "Really? I told her I had two jobs. She never mentioned she had three. Damn she's really something."

He was impressed. The admiration was obvious in his eyes. As it fucking should be. He was smart. Any smart man would ask Beulah out. She probably got asked out a lot.

"Did she say yes?" I asked.

"Are you fucking kidding me right now?" Stone growled beside me. "What is wrong with you? Jesus she's the help."

"You need better friends," the bartender said and Stone ignored him. He wasn't one to get worked up over other's opinions.

"I'm going to find her." I didn't have to explain myself. Stone would bitch about it, reminding me why I shouldn't run after her, and he would be right. But I was going after her anyway. She'd been upset by something Stone had said. I knew he did.

"Whatever," was Stone's response.

I was almost to the door when the caterer came walking out with food instead of Beulah. She paused when she saw me. "Is something wrong Mr. Van Allan?"

"Where's Beulah?"

The lady frowned. "I sent her to change shoes."

Change shoes? "Why?"

She didn't look very pleased with me but she was trying to hide it. "Because the shoes that have been provided for her uniform are two sizes too small. She's struggling to walk around."

Holy hell! That was why she was limping. Motherfucker! Why didn't she said something? "Where is she?" I asked, walking inside not waiting for a reply.

"Her room, I believe, sir," I heard the her say as I stalked through the house to the stairs leading to the room she slept in.

I should have asked her this morning when I saw her limping. I'd been so wrapped up in keeping my distance that I ignored it. She hadn't said anything. How long had she been wearing shoes that were too small? Was this something Portia did? I had more damn shoes than any man needed, and she was walking around in cheap tennis shoes that didn't even fit her. This was why I wasn't good for her. I was selfish and self-involved. She needed protecting and someone to care for her.

The bartender, however, wasn't good enough. He couldn't take care of her the way she needed. He was a fucking bartender. Frustrated with my thoughts, I jerked the door open and started down the stairs.

"Hello?" Beulah's voice sounded worried. No one ever came down here I assumed.

"It's me," I told her as I reached the bottom step and turned right into the room where her bed sat along with the washer and dryer.

She was standing with one shoe in her hand and one shoe on her foot. Her eyes were wide with what looked like worry. "I was coming right back. I just needed to change shoes."

At seeing me, her first thought was to explain herself. As if she'd done something wrong. What kind of monster did she think I was? Had I acted in a way that she expected me to yell at her over changing her shoes?

"How long have you been wearing shoes that are too small?" I asked turning my attention to her feet.

She curled her toes under on her barefoot but I could see

the blisters and what looked like bruises. My stomach felt sick. I'd been letting her walk around all day, working to get ready for tonight so I could entertain a bunch of my friends while her feet looked like this.

"For a while," she said her voice was just above a whisper.

"How long?" I repeated.

She sighed. "Since I started working here."

Almost seven months. She'd been working in those shoes for almost seven months. "Why? Did Portia not ask your shoe size?" Portia was a lot of things but cruel to employees wasn't one of them. Indifferent, yes, but not cruel.

"They were new. She'd just bought them for Ms. Charlotte before she quit. They're part of the uniform. She asked me if they would work and I said yes. She said I could buy some if not. I didn't have money for that. I was making sure Heidi was taken care of so I kept putting it off. Thinking I'd break them in."

Rage, frustration, and something else pounded in my head. She was the most selfless person I knew. She didn't deserve this— this shit life she'd been given—but she smiled and lived it happily. I listened to people bitch about their investments and the pressure their parents put on them and not fucking being able to travel when they wanted to. And here was Beulah doing all she could to take care of someone else, never complaining.

I pointed at the bathtub. "Get in there. Soak. Rest your feet. I'll get you some ointment and bandages and soft socks. But for now, relax. Use some fucking bubbles. Take a long time."

"Your party, Monique needs me up there. She gave me shoes that fit—"

"Beulah. Don't. I need you to get your sweet little ass in that tub and take a motherfucking bubble bath. A long one. I need you to get off your feet and pamper them. Or I'm going to lose my goddamn mind."

She stood there frozen. We stared at each other and her eyes looked like they were damp. I didn't think I could take it if she cried. I was holding on by a thread. I wanted to undress her and put her in that tub myself. I wanted to bath her and touch her and smell her because I'd let myself sink. She was impossible not to love. How was I supposed to fight this?

"I'm going to get you some things. You're going to bath while I'm gone. I'll be back down in an hour with the things I said. You just . . . please just soak in that tub. Do you have body wash? Bubble bath?"

She shook her head slowly. "I have a bar of soap."

"Let me get that. Don't get in there yet. Unless you want me to come down here and see you naked. If that's the case, I won't argue."

Her cheeks flushed, and she ducked her head. "I'll wait."

I was able to laugh then. Not a deep laugh because my heart was hurting so damn much right now that laughing seemed unnatural. But I did laugh. "I'll be right back. Take off that other shoe."

I didn't wait for her to argue again. I went upstairs to get her some things that would ease her pain and make her more comfortable. I'd take all that expensive shit that Portia had upstairs she'd shipped in from France. Beulah could have as many baths as she wanted.

Chapter Twenty-Three

BEULAH

THE SMELL THAT filled the room was heavenly. I knew this was Portia's bath supplies just like I knew the large white luxurious towel was one from her master bath. I had been sitting on the bed with bare feet when Jasper came back downstairs carrying a basket full of bath items, a pair of soft plush socks, bandages, and ointment. He'd handed it to me and said, "Please use all of this." That had been it. He didn't say anything else before he left.

I was worried about Monique and Jerry handling the crowd upstairs, but Jasper had been very clear he didn't want me going back up there. I didn't know how he found out about the shoes for sure, but my guess was Monique told him. She was very unhappy about the situation when I explained. It wasn't Jasper's fault. I was the one who didn't buy new shoes that fit.

Slowly, I eased into the water wincing when the warm water covered my feet. I sank down into the bubbles and leaned back against the porcelain. I always took showers. I'd never soaked in a bath here. I had when I lived at home. Mom had a bathtub in her bathroom and every once in a while, I'd go put some shampoo in the running water to make bubbles and enjoy a bath. This reminded me of those times.

Nothing about those baths compared to this. I hadn't met Jasper then. My mom was still alive and I was safe. I wasn't alone. Although tonight, for a moment, I hadn't felt alone. Jasper had cared. He was upset, but he had cared. He didn't want to see me in pain. I closed my eyes and listened for the music and footsteps upstairs. I felt guilty about not helping Monique. I hoped Jasper got her some help.

I couldn't hear the music though. It was quiet up here. The footsteps had slowed to almost nothing. I wondered if they had taken the food outside for the last time and started to pack up. The night was still early. I didn't think they'd stop serving food so soon.

Because of my stubbornness about the shoes, I'd let Jasper down tonight. He'd helped me so much and I had to sit down because of those stupid shoes. Tomorrow I'd buy new ones. I had sent the ones Monique gave me back upstairs with Jasper. He didn't want me leaving this room tonight or walking around.

Within the hour that I soaked in the bathtub, the entire upstairs had become silent. The water had cooled, so I stepped out of the tub and wrapped myself in the towel that he'd brought me. Every time I washed and folded these towels I had wondered how they must feel to use after a bath. They were the softest, fluffiest towels I'd ever seen. Now I knew how luxurious they were. They were very close to being magical. I ran the tip of my nose over the delicate cotton and inhaled.

This was really nice. I didn't need to get used to it, but right now I would enjoy it. Putting on my pajamas didn't seem as appealing as it normally did. So, I sat down on the bed still wrapped in the towel and took a few more minutes indulging because when I took this towel off, I was washing it and never using one of these again. This wasn't my life. I was a cheap thin towel kind of girl. Towels were to get dry and nothing more. Wanting and desiring this kind of pampering was a waste of my time. But for just a few more seconds, I pretended like it was okay.

The moments ticked by, and I finally stood up and took the towel off. I went over to the suitcase that held my belongings at the foot of the bed and pulled out clean panties and the faded pink pajamas I'd had since Momma had given them to me for Christmas when I was sixteen. Heidi had a matching pair. I had a picture of us in front of the tree wearing these pajamas. Heidi loved it when Momma had given us matching pajamas for Christmas. She did it every few years when she could afford it. Because these were the last we had gotten, I cherished them. Sleeping in them made her feel close to me.

I packed all the bath items back in the basket and put the towel in the washing machine. Then I sat down and bandaged my feet. The ointment soothed them, and the bath had helped immensely.

After that was all taken care of, I looked toward the stairs and thought about going up to check on things. Then I looked at my feet and slipped the socks on. Jasper had asked me not to walk around on them. So I didn't.

The footsteps on the stairs surprised me and I sat back up from having just laid down.

"You dressed?" Jasper asked.

I hadn't expected him again.

"Yes," I replied refusing to be embarrassed by my pajamas. I loved them. I didn't care if they were worn and faded. I didn't care what Jasper thought. At least, I didn't want to care. That counted for something.

He came around the corner carrying a cup of tea and a plate of food. "Thought you might be hungry."

"Thank you, but you've got company. A lot of it. You don't have to keep leaving them to come check on me."

"Everyone is gone. I ended the party early and cleared the place out. We have a large portion of leftovers so there is no need for you to cook the next couple of days. The caterer left instructions on how to heat things up."

Now I felt even worse. "I am so sorry, Jasper. I should have gotten shoes before now. I ruined your party."

He sat the plate down on the table beside my bed. "I didn't want to have that party. It was pointless and annoying. I forced myself to have the party. I wanted to convince myself it was what I wanted. It used to be what I wanted. But things have changed."

He didn't look happy about that change. "Work? Is it more than you wanted?" I asked.

The corner of his mouth tilted up as he looked at me. "Yeah. It is."

I nodded my head in understanding. "What would make you happy then if not a party?" I wanted him to be happy. It was odd how that had become important to me. I just didn't know what to do to make him happy.

"Something I don't deserve."

That wasn't really an answer. I waited, thinking he'd say more but he didn't.

"Eat that. Get full. Rest. And don't come upstairs early. Sleep in. You'll have new tennis shoes when you get up. I'm sending for them in the morning. And some socks. Good thick socks. The kind that feel so damn good you don't want to take them off."

I laughed. "Okay. But I have socks. You don't have to get those."

"You don't have these socks. You need them."

I started to say something else about not needing socks and he cut me off. "Beulah, if you're about to argue with me don't bother. Let me buy the socks. I may need to buy the whole damn store out. I need something to make this ache in my chest at the sight of your feet go away."

My heart squeezed, and then did a little flutter. He was making this worse. My feelings for him were growing. I wanted to tell him he needed to stop this. Stop being so kind. But I couldn't. "Okay. Thank you."

He gave me a relieved smile. "Goodnight, Beulah."

"Goodnight," I replied.

Then I watched him leave. Long after he was gone and the food was finished, I laid in bed with a smile. Because being in love wasn't all bad. Sometimes it felt like warm sunshine.

Chapter Twenty-Four

JASPER

"YOU'RE MAKING A mistake."

Stone was probably right. I just didn't give a shit. I had fought this all I could. Last night when I'd heard the bartender asked her out, I'd immediately been jealous. Then I saw her feet and it was painful. Seeing her hurt physically pained me.

"I bought her shoes. She needed them," I told him getting some cheese from the party last night out of the fridge.

"She's asleep. Because you told her to sleep in. She's an employee and you're not treating her like one. You're blurring the lines. It's a fucking nightmare waiting to happen."

I wasn't going to do anything to hurt her. "I'm helping her. She's hurt, and I am showing compassion. Get some. It'll do your cold heart good."

"This isn't about fucking compassion. It's about you being attracted to her. I get that. She's gorgeous and has the whole damsel in distress, sweet thing, going for her. You like to save people.

It's that damn heart of yours being too big. But this time, you're dancing too close to the flame and you need to back the hell up."

I was past the being too close to the flame. I'd been consumed. It had taken me under last night. No need to tell him that though. It would just send him over the top. "Are you hungry? We've got some good stuff in here," I said changing the subject.

"What the fuck ever," he said with frustration. "I can't save you from yourself. I don't have the time to try. I'm going to go get the shit done that needs done, then I need some space. You jump off that cliff if you want to. But while you're making mistakes, try not to crush her in the meantime. She's not like the others. Which is why you're so damn attracted to her."

I finished getting food out of the fridge and didn't respond. When he turned to leave, I spoke up. "I won't hurt her."

He paused but didn't look back at me. "You won't mean to." Then he left.

I stared at the door that led to her room downstairs. Last night, I had checked out the yellow guest bedroom and thought about moving her up there. Near me. In a real bedroom with a real bathroom. Before I had finally fallen asleep, I'd decided it was a good idea.

In the light of day, I wasn't so sure. If I was going to blur the lines, it was better to just erase them. Could I do that though? She needed saving. She needed someone to depend on.

I wanted to be that someone. It had been a long time since I wanted that. Maisie had been every nightmare a relationship could be. She was exactly like my mother. Selfish, vain, demanding, and a cheater. She needed men to want her. She was completely fucked in the head. When she'd broken things off she wanted me to beg her not to. She had wanted me to grovel.

I had felt like throwing a motherfucking party. Being free of her and the life I didn't want with her was the best thing that had happened to me in a while. Coming back here hadn't been so bad until I had to see my mother.

"I didn't set my alarm. I slept later than I thought I would." Beulah's voice was soft and slightly husky from sleep. I had been so deep in my thoughts I hadn't heard her come up the stairs.

"You needed the rest," I looked down to see she was still wearing the socks I had brought her last night. "I got you some new shoes and socks as promised. But until you have to go somewhere just wear the socks. You look good in them."

She glanced at her feet and laughed. "Thanks. I think."

"Sit. I'll fix you something to eat. There's a ton of food in the fridge that the caterers left."

Her head snapped back up and she looked at me with wide eyes. "You can't fix me food. That's my job."

"I'm the boss. I can do whatever I want. And I want to fix you breakfast."

The soft smile on her face should have scared me. It should have been a warning. But I wanted it. I wanted her. I didn't give a fuck about our impossible situation. "Fine then. I'm starving," she said as she walked over and sat on one of the stools at the bar.

"Did you sleep good?" I asked.

I wasn't sure what she liked to eat. So I made her a plate of everything I put on mine.

"Yes. Thank you. For the shoes and socks. I should have bought some before now."

The uniform was Portia's doing, so she should have supplied shoes that fit correctly. I didn't point that out though. I didn't want to talk about Portia. She wasn't here and for once I was at peace being home.

"How's Heidi?" I asked instead.

"Better! I talked to her yesterday. She feels good and was cleared to go to the crafts room yesterday. That's all she could talk about. Well that, and she asked if I could bring cupcakes today. I have them tucked away in the fridge."

"You should take her some of the sweets that are left from the party."

"Thank you. She'd like that."

The love in her voice was real. That was what I imagined families should be like. I was an only child and my parents were never around when I was growing up. My friends all had similar lives. But what Beulah had was what I wanted as a kid. I wanted that unconditional love. I bet her mother was everything to her. I knew Heidi was. She had unconditional love from Heidi, and she gave in return.

"What was your mother like?" I asked before I thought that through. She may not be ready to talk about her mother. I didn't look up as I back pedaled. "I'm sorry, I didn't think before I spoke. You're . . . I just thought . . . I was wondering if she looked like you." I almost said she was the most unique female I'd ever met. That had to be something her mother gave her.

Beulah smiled. It was a sad smile. Her eyes held memories I would never be privy to. They were good ones and I was envious of that. Even if she'd had to suffer the pain of that loss, she had memories that I never would have.

"She was amazing. I'm not saying that because she's gone either. If she were still here I'd say the same. She worked so hard all day long our entire lives, but somehow managed to cook family dinners we ate together. When we were old enough to stand in chairs, she let us cook with her. Heidi helped too. She would wash vegetables or put the noodles in water to boil. Mom never acted like she was different. I don't think Heidi knew she was until she started school. Even though she had to take care of Heidi she always made me feel just as special. I don't know how she managed it. Doing it all alone, she gave us memories of lemonade popsicles on hot summer days outside, running through the sprinkler. I don't think she ever got any sleep, but she always had time. Always had a smile. I never once saw her sad. She cried at my high school graduation, but they were happy tears she said. I think she was the most perfect human on this earth."

Beulah's eyes literally glowed with love when she spoke. I was almost jealous of her life and of a mom like that. But it was Beulah. I liked knowing she and Heidi had grown up like that. It explained a lot about her. I'd never met a girl like her because I didn't know one with a life like hers.

"She sounds perfect."

"She was . . . and thanks for asking. I miss talking about her. I think about her all the time. But I never get to talk about her. I'm afraid it will upset Heidi. She doesn't understand completely, and she misses her too. So it's . . . nice. Great actually. That felt good. She needs to be remembered."

The tears that hadn't fallen collected in her eyes and she gave me a wobbly smile. Again, I didn't think. I found myself not thinking with her a lot, I just acted. Reaching over I pulled her into my arms and held her. She came willingly. Her arms wrapped around my neck and she laid her head on my shoulder. Nothing had ever felt this right. The missing piece I was always searching for clicked into place. And I was terrified.

Chapter Twenty-Five
BEULAH

SOMETHING HAD HAPPENED. It was different. Jasper had let me go, moved back and said he need to be somewhere and left. Was I not supposed to hug him back? I wasn't sure. But talking to him about Mom had made me feel vulnerable. Open. I'd shared with him not only Heidi, but now my mom. It had felt good to be held and not feel alone

But he'd all but ran from me.

I had stood there unsure what to think or do for a few minutes, then I'd gone to work cleaning up our breakfast plates.

Putting on my new shoes, I sighed at how good they felt. It was time to leave to see Heidi. I had her to look forward to today. Thinking about Jasper was pointless.

When I was unlocking my car to get inside, Stone pulled into the drive. His black Range Rover was dangerous and expensive— just like him, I assumed. I didn't wait around to speak to him since he wasn't one to converse with me. Unless he needed me to do something. Or to warn me to stay in my place.

I quickly put the cupcakes and other treats I'd chosen for Heidi and May in the back seat. Before I could climb inside my car, he was out of his and he stopped me. "Not working today?"

I sighed. As if this was his business. "It's Sunday. My day off."

"You got last night off."

My hand tightened its grip on the door frame. He was so frustrating. He also had to be the angriest most unhappy human I knew. "I didn't ask for that. I need Sundays though. I visit my sister."

Stone didn't seem to care or understand. I wondered if he was this cold with the world. Or was it just me that he hated?

"I'm not your boss."

"We agree on something," I replied before I could bite my tongue.

I winced and a tug on the corner of his mouth caused me to pause. In shock. Had he been on the verge of a smile? The scowl he always had was back, and I figured I must have confused his facial expression. I didn't wait around for more small talk. I got into the car and closed the door. He stood there in his jeans, black T-shirt and sunglasses with his arms crossed over his chest looking like some dark sexy god. That was annoying.

The drive to Among the Spanish Moss was easy. There was never much traffic on Sunday mornings. Walking into the building, I took the plate I had made for the staff there and dropped it off at the front desk.

"Good morning, Beulah. I've been looking forward to your visit all morning. We love these treats." Tammy was about fifty, had three grandchildren, and moved here from Nebraska ten years ago to be near her youngest daughter. She was also one of

Heidi's favorites.

"I added a little extra in there with the cupcakes. Y'all enjoy them," I told her. "Better go find my girl. She's ready for cupcakes too I imagine."

Tammy laughed. "Oh, yes. She's come by three times already this morning to tell me you were coming with cupcakes."

"Beulah!" Heidi's voice rang down the hall.

"Guess she was headed back for her fourth visit," I said, then waved goodbye to Tammy and headed to meet my sister. Her smile always cheered me up.

"May is in the activity room. We got to get her," Heidi told me as I reached her. She clapped her hands when she saw the treats I was carrying. "Oh boy! May's gonna be so happy."

"Then let's get her and find a spot for a picnic. We will eat dessert first."

Heidi giggled with delight. "I love you, Beulah."

"I love you more."

She didn't argue. She was too excited about the picnic and desserts. We collected May from the activity room and made our way outside. Heidi told me all about the game of soccer they played yesterday and how May scored the winning goal. May blushed a lot and then gave me a bashful hug once I put the treats down on the grassy spot under the tree they picked out.

"I missed you," May said sweetly.

"I missed you too," I assured her.

May and Heidi both took a cupcake. The cupcakes were pink today, sprinkled with Skittles. Heidi loved Skittles and squealed when she saw them. "It's like my birthday. But it's really Vern's birthday. I should save him a cupcake."

I didn't know Vern, but I nodded in agreement.

"You have new shoes," May noticed. "They're pretty."

"Yes, I do. My others were too small."

May frowned. "My feet stopped growing."

"They're supposed to. Mine did too. Those shoes were too little all along."

She nodded but she didn't seem convinced.

"Can we play soccer today?" Heidi asked.

"Of course. I want to see May show us some of her fancy footwork."

May lit up. She was proud of herself.

"Yeah!" Heidi agreed happy to cheer her friend on. "Where is your boyfriend?"

Her question startled me. "My who?"

"Your boyfriend that came this week when I was sick."

Jasper. "Oh, that's my boss. Remember? He's not my boyfriend. I don't have a boyfriend."

Heidi grinned. "He is too. He's handsome. He smiles at you a lot and he likes to look at you."

I didn't know what to say to that. "He does?" I asked.

Heidi nodded, and then she and May giggled. "Beulah has a boyfriend," they began to sing over and over.

I wouldn't be able to ever bring Jasper back. Heidi would be sure to mention this to him. I just laughed at their silliness and ate another cupcake. The warm sunshine had a cool breeze that made it a perfect day to enjoy outdoors.

Momma would have loved today. She always took us outside to spend our Sundays. Picnics and treats. She'd be happy Heidi lived here, and that Heidi had a place where she fit. Where she had friends. I was thankful I was going to be able to keep her here. This was a life for Heidi. One where she fit in and she had security.

"I wish you were here, Momma," I whispered before getting up and following the girls out to the open field where the soccer nets were. They were inviting others to play and the excitement of the game was obvious.

My weirdness with Jasper was soon forgotten.

Chapter Twenty-Six

JASPER

THE WHISKEY BOTTLE in front of me had started out as a way to get my mind off Beulah, and with each glass things became clearer. Now I'd almost had a fifth of whiskey and I knew I was drunk. I should go to my bedroom to sleep it off, but I didn't. I waited for her. I had to see her and explain about this morning. About how fucking scared I'd been.

Stone had left after we argued again. He said he'd be back in a week and that he had his own shit to deal with. Which I understood. He was running from his father and the Richmond department stores and malls all over the goddamn country that would one day be his. I didn't know why, but Stone hated the man who would give him his fortune. Just last month, he talked about running off and joining the rodeo circuit, which was a crock of shit. Hilarious, and a crock of shit. He'd grown up much the same way I had, and neither of us was getting on some crazy as hell bull.

I was either more intoxicated than I assumed, or so lost in

thought I wasn't listening, but Beulah entered the room without me realizing it.

"Jasper?" Her voice was unsure. Sweet and kind.

"You're back. Have a good visit?"

She hesitated. I assumed she saw the whiskey bottle. I sat there with my full glass. "Yes. It was nice. They enjoyed the other treats you told me to take."

How did I do this? How did I love her? How did I do it and not hurt her? Could I? She was so damn sweet. I was scared I would mess up. Fuck that. What if she saw me for who I was and left me? How would I survive?

"Shit," I muttered.

"What?"

I sat my glass down and laid my head back closing my eyes. Not looking at her was easier. I couldn't face what I was about to say while I admitted it. Because that's why I'd stayed up. To tell her before I lost her.

"Do you know why I ran out this morning?" I asked her. Hell, she may have this all figured out by now anyway.

"No," was her uneasy response. This was making her nervous. I didn't want to do that.

"I left because I was fucking terrified," I admitted.

She didn't say anything. I heard her shuffle her feet. I continued. "You scare me. I've never been scared before. Not about women. But you, Beulah Edwards, scare the fuck out of me."

"Oh," her voice was soft and she sounded confused. I didn't have to see her face to know that. She still had no idea.

"I don't fall in love. Not my thing. I had parents who hated each other. I figured they must have been in love once. And saw what love had done to them. Hell, I could be just like my dad and fall in love with someone as fucking cruel and cold as my mother. I stayed clear of having feelings for a girl and it was easy. It was easy . . . until you. And you didn't even try. You were just you and I have fallen so hard that I can't believe it myself. You're different," I said opening my eyes and turning my head to look directly at her. "You are the different, the special that breaks a man. Makes him want more. Makes him want a life he thought he'd never have. Until you, I never wanted to love someone, Beulah. But you . . . I want to love you. I think I've waited my whole life to love you."

Her eyes were wide, her mouth slightly open in surprise or shock. She was frozen in place. Not moving. It looked as if she were barely breathing. If she ran from me or she didn't want this, I'd suffer. I had gotten my stupid ass drunk and thrown myself out there to be trampled.

"Me?" she finally said just above a whisper.

There it was again. The thing that made her different. If I had told this to any other girl I'd ever dated she would have immediately taken what I'd said and ran. Gotten all she could out of me. But Beulah just stood there. Unable to move. Wondering if I meant to say all this to her.

"Yes. You. I don't think it could ever be anyone else."

She blinked and touched her temple, rubbing her forehead with her hand, then she shook her head. "Are you drunk?"

I laughed then. She made me laugh a lot. Something I needed. I wanted to be close to her for many reasons, but her joy about life was part of it. She made me happy. I'd been pretending so damn long, I had forgotten what real happiness felt like. She knew though. She found it even when life sucked.

"Yes, I'm drunk. But everything I just said is why I'm drunk. I can't stop thinking about you. I can't stop wanting to be near you.

I gave you a job in my office so you'd be close to me during the day. Even when I acted like a dick it was because I was attracted to you and I didn't want to be. Then I spent more time with you, got to know you, and it was more than your beautiful face. It was your beautiful soul." I wondered if I'd be coming up with such fucking great prose if I was sober. I doubted it. I'd be so damn nervous I wouldn't say half this shit. I meant it. Every word. The words flowed easily with the alcohol involved.

She still wasn't moving. So I got up and walked over to stand in front of her. Close enough that I could feel her warmth, but not touch her. She tilted her head back to look up at me. "I-I love you too. But . . . we can't do that. Love each other. When you're sober you will realize that. This," she looked around her. "We live two different lives in two different worlds. That won't mix."

I had tried to tell myself that. Stone had tried to fucking drill it into my head. But if life only gives you a Beulah once . . . how do you walk away? I didn't want to be my dad. I didn't want his unhappy life. I wanted a life with sunshine in it. A life with Beulah. "Let me show you I can make this work. Please. I can't just let you slip through my fingers. I'm lucky enough to have found you. I won't find another girl like you. And in this life, I need you. I'll do everything I can to make you need me."

She blinked again, and sighed. Her eyes were damp. "I don't believe this is happening. I'm afraid to believe it. When you wake up tomorrow you're going to regret you said all this. It'll be awkward and . . . I need this job. Both jobs."

I reached out and put my hand on her waist, gently tugging her to me. "I won't change my mind. And I sure as hell won't regret this. Let me hold you tonight. When you wake up in my arms you'll know it's going to be okay. We found each other for a reason. It was fate. It's supposed to be. We're supposed to be."

She was stiff, but with my words she slowly eased and relaxed. Her body molded against mine. "I think fate sometimes can be cruel," she whispered against my chest.

"I won't let fate hurt you. I swear."

Chapter Twenty-Seven

BEULAH

I HAD BEEN in this room many times to clean it. Now I stood in Jasper's massive bathroom with a towel around me after taking a bath and looked at myself in the mirror. Was I making a mistake? He was drunk. I could smell the whiskey on his breath. But he'd also been very serious. He hadn't tried anything. He had said words, such beautiful words. Words that a drunk mind doesn't just make up, right?

"You okay in there?" his voice came from his bedroom. He wasn't passed out. He was waiting on me.

"Yes."

He didn't say more. I slipped on my pink pajamas and looked at myself one last time in the mirror. My ratty pajamas weren't exactly something a woman wore to attract a man. But we were just sleeping . . . in his bed . . . together. I should have said no. I should have gone to my room.

But I wanted this. Jasper. Us.

This was a gamble. Maybe the biggest of my life. I couldn't let Heidi be affected though. If he changed his mind would I lose my jobs? Could I let my heart guide me when I had a sister to take care of?

I opened the door and was going to tell him my concerns. My worries. Because he needed to understand how this was more than me taking a chance. I had much more at stake than my heart. I was barely through the door, and he was there. In front of me. His body was warm and his hands cupped my face. Those eyes of his that had been breathtaking the first time I saw him study me. They were open. Clear. I could see the raw emotion in them. This was a chance for him too. One that obviously scared him.

I started to ask why when his mouth covered mine and he pressed me back against the door I'd just walked out of. I'd never been kissed quite like this. It was heady and delicious. The taste of the whiskey he'd drunk was dark and wicked. I closed my eyes, and wrapped my arms around his neck. I forgot everything I'd been worried about, and soaked in the smell of him. I reveled at the way his body made mine tingle with excitement.

Our tongues danced and our breath mingled in the dark room lit only by the moonlight streaming through the windows. I was hidden here. We were alone, and my body was humming with need. A need that demanded more. I pressed closer to him. My fingers laced through his hair and he made a low sound that vibrated his chest.

His mouth left mine and trailed kisses down my neck, then my feet were off the ground. I was in his arms as he walked the distance to his bed and laid me down gently. His shirt was off in an instant, and all he wore was a pair of shorts that hung loosely on his hips. He was beautiful. I lifted my eyes to his as he moved over me, caging me in. The softness of the bed was under me, and his hard, chiseled body was on top.

My back arched as his tongue traced my collarbone. Jasper unbuttoned my top just enough that he could kiss to the tops of my breasts. Then he looked up and into my eyes. His eyes burned as brightly as my body. "I won't do more. I'll go slow. I'll be sober when I'm inside you. But I just want to taste, to feel a little."

The idea of him being inside me caused me to shiver. My body felt a tightness of anticipation. But I wanted him sober too. "Okay," I said breathlessly.

He rested his head on my shoulder then lowered his body until I could feel the hardness of his arousal between my legs. We were separated by clothing but the pressure made me squirm.

"Feel good?" he asked, his voice a dark whisper in my ear.

"Yes," I admitted. There was no denying I wanted this.

He pressed and rocked against me and on impulse I grabbed his arms and moved with him. The friction from his body felt better than the actual one experience I'd had with sex. Then I'd been nervous and scared. Unsure. Now I ached with the tease of real pleasure. This was Jasper. I loved him. Maybe that was the difference.

His breath was hot against my neck as his hand slid down my body, over my hips and down to my thigh to pull my leg up high against his hip. He continued working his body against mine and the deep sound of his groan almost made me climax.

"I want inside you so fucking bad," he said. His face was buried in my hair. His breathing becoming as erratic as mine. "I've got to stop. But I want you to come for me. Can I make you come for me?"

If I didn't come, I might explode. I nodded my head because

I couldn't say words. Not at that moment.

He moved off me, and I started to grab him to bring him back. But his hand slipped under my pajama bottoms and he lifted his head until his eyes locked with mine. My body went still and I could barely breath. I began to pant as he eased his hand under the silk of my panties until his fingers slid between the wetness of my folds. My body took over then, and I jerked in response.

"Fuck, you're soaking," he said, his eyes dark as he watched me. He entered me then. One finger at first, then two. Slowly pumping to delay the build. I couldn't keep my eyes open. My head fell back, and my body took over, climbing toward that pleasure it knew was coming. I grabbed at his chest, my nails raking down. His mouth hoovered over my neck as his tongue flicked at my heated skin.

"Please," I begged because I had to get there. I needed him to go faster. Harder.

"Enjoy it," he said as he pressed deeper. I began to tremble as he held back from pushing me over the edge. My head tossed back and forth against the pillow and I cried out as the clawing need inside me grew.

Just when I was about to beg him again, his thumb pressed my clit with the right amount of pressure and his fingers slammed into me in one move.

"Oh, God!" I cried out and the world exploded around me. The electricity of an orgasm given to me by a man I loved. An orgasm I didn't give myself. The strength of it rocked my body so hard I lost my breath. I was okay like this. Lost in this world floating from a high that had been amazing. And he'd only used his hand.

He pulled me into his arms and rolled to his side taking me

with him. I floated down from my euphoria, wrapped in his embrace. His breath on my neck and his smell all around me.

Exhaustion from the day and the experience took over, and I let myself relax and trust this. Trust him. I didn't bring up my concerns. I wasn't sure I needed to because this felt right. It was safe . . . I felt safe. The way he held me against him I didn't feel alone. Not anymore. No words were spoken by either of us, but we didn't need any words. Moments came in life that you didn't question. I hadn't had many, but this was one.

It was a terrible idea, but a perfect one all the same. Loving Jasper would be the easiest thing I had ever done. Was it fair not to take a chance on love? I saw his heart. He was good. He was trustworthy. He wasn't going to destroy me and leave me unable to take care of Heidi. His heart was too big for that. This wasn't a mistake. It couldn't be.

My eyes fluttered open slowly and I turned my head to look up at him. His eyes were closed. Long eyelashes fanned his cheekbones. Perfect cheekbones. He didn't have a flaw. It was the man inside, the one overcoming his own pain that I loved. He was so much more than a spoiled rich kid. He was a fighter, and I respected that. If I didn't, I couldn't have fallen in love with him.

Chapter Twenty-Eight

JASPER

I HAD STEPPED over the line. No, I'd blown the line completely away. There was no line anymore. It had taken the whiskey to push me over, but I would have eventually done it anyway.

There was no keeping Beulah at arm's length. I didn't want her at arm's length. I wanted Beulah right where she was at this moment. In my arms. Asleep, looking so damn beautiful it hurt.

We had to figure this all out now. Find a way to make it all work. Because I wanted this. I might have been drunk last night, but I'd been honest. Being with her made me happy. Happier than I could ever remember. I was willing to do anything to be with her.

I needed to prepare myself for her arguments, though. She wouldn't be okay with moving out of the basement. I knew that was going to be the first issue. But I wasn't going to sleep up here in this bed knowing she was down there with the washing machine. I'd sleep with her if she refused. That should fix that.

Stone would be a problem when he returned. I'd have to

talk to him. Make sure he changed his attitude with her. I wasn't going to allow him to talk down to her any longer. I hated he did it before. I'd let it slide for selfish reasons. Mostly because I knew the affect Stone had on females. He'd been able to charm women his entire life. I was afraid if he were nice to Beulah she'd fall under the spell he so easily cast when he wanted to.

Maisie and I had ended things after I found her coming on to Stone in her bra and panties. He'd been turning her down of course, but she'd been after him. That was the last straw for both of us. She wasn't the first girl in my past to want Stone.

He was my best friend, and not once had he ever taken one of my girlfriends up on their flirting and propositions. He'd ignored their advances and been cruel until they were gone from my life. Once he knew they would cheat, he made sure to make their lives hell. I never realized what he was doing until it was done.

Beulah was different though. She was nothing like the others. He didn't need to mistreat her. She would never come on to him. She was here. Tucked against me, trusting me. I had the power to hurt her, and not just her heart, but through her income. She loved Heidi above all else. And she trusted me even with that. It was humbling.

When I had started drinking last night I'd thought that her fear for Heidi's security might be the reason I could never have her. That she'd not let us have more. That all I would ever get was a good employee and possibly a friendship.

She'd surprised me. With that trust she'd handed over, I would make sure that she was taken care of. Heidi would never be without her home. And Beulah would be secure in that. I'd handle it today. I could pay in advance for the next ten years. It would ease any concerns or fears Beulah might harbor.

We would be free to enjoy this. I'd found her and I wanted it all with her.

Beulah stirred in my arms and I watched as her eyes slowly blinked open. A sleepy smile spread across her face as she stretched and stared up at me. "So that wasn't a dream," she said in a voice thick from sleep.

"It was very real," I assured her, bending to kiss her nose.

She turned closer and buried her head in my chest. "How can this work?"

"When you're in love, you find a way. We can work it out together. Starting with my handling your worries about Heidi. I'm going to pay for her care, ten years in advance today." Before I could say more, Beulah's head shot up and she looked at me like I'd lost my mind.

"What? You can't do that . . . that's a fortune!"

"I'm sure they'll give me a discount. Although I don't care about the cost. I want Heidi taken care of regardless of what happens with us. I don't intend to let you go, but if you ever want to walk away, I want you to have that freedom. I don't want you staying with me because you are scared of losing your employment. I want you to want me. Because God knows I don't want to think about life without you."

Beulah sat up and pushed her hair back out of her face with both hands, then pulled her knees up to her chest and wrapped her arms around them. "Jasper, that's not okay. I mean the idea of Heidi's care and home being secure is . . . completely amazing. But it is a fairy tale. I don't live in that world. And just because we," she paused and looked at me. "We are doing this, and that's my gamble to take. You shouldn't have to pay me to have me in your life. That's . . . well, it's wrong. It's unfair."

Every girl before her had started expecting gifts. Expensive gifts, trips, and luxury from me the moment we got together. I wasn't offering Beulah any of that. Just security for her sister. And this was her response. Would it always be like this? Would she make me love her more every day? I was going to be so damn wrapped up in her that I'd have to make sure she never left me. I had a taste of her and I wanted to hold on tight.

"Beulah, do you love me?" I asked her although she had already told me she did.

"Yes."

"Then let me do this. Let me give Heidi security. To make us work, we need to make some changes. You not killing yourself with three jobs is one of those changes. I will take care of Heidi. You can work with me at the office and I'm going to get another housekeeper to work here. And before you say anything, let me finish. You are with me now. We are a couple. I don't want to see you cleaning my house. I want to sit with you at night and watch movies, talk, make love. I want to watch you eat breakfast and enjoy you. If you're waiting on me it's going to kill me. I love you. Please give us a chance."

She laid her forehead on her knees that were tucked up close to her chin and closed her eyes. I saw her sigh, and I waited. She needed a moment to process. I gave it to her.

My heart was pounding in my chest as the seconds ticked by. Beulah was independent. She was proud. She didn't want to take any help from me. She wanted to work for what she got. She had a beautiful heart, but if we were going to make this work, we had to make some changes.

"The job I do at the office isn't enough. I need to do more," she said without looking up at me.

"I have another position I need filled. I want a private secretary. The one we have now isn't exclusively mine. I've been hesitant to hire one because I needed someone I could put up with for long hours, and be able to work with one-on-one. You'd be the perfect answer to that. The position would come with a salary and benefits."

I had already thought of this. I just hadn't planned on laying it on her this soon. But it seemed like the right moment.

She finally lifted her head and sighed again. Her shoulders rising and falling in one heavy breath. "Okay. If that will help you. Then okay. I want us to work too. I just don't want to be a leech. I need to make my own money. Help pay the bills and for food."

There was no way on earth I was letting her pay the bills or for food, but we'd deal with that later. I didn't want to argue all morning. "Good."

"Most people don't start a relationship living together," she said frowning.

"Yes, but we were living in the same house before we started a relationship. Different rules." I wasn't about to let her get the idea she needed to move out.

She leaned over and rested her head on my shoulder. Nothing was said. I held her and we watched the early morning sun through the windows.

This was what I wanted and I finally had it.

Chapter Twenty-Nine
BEULAH

THE EASIEST THING I'd done today was quit my job at the club. I'd barely been an employee there. I felt guilty about that. However, they hadn't seemed to care that I wasn't coming back.

The hardest thing I'd done today was move my things upstairs. Jasper had given me the yellow guest bedroom across from his. He said I wouldn't be sleeping in there but he wanted me to have my own space. He was trying to make our relationship easy on me.

Every time I had thought about Heidi and that she was going to be taken care of for the next ten years, the relief I felt almost brought me to tears. No more worrying if she was going to have to leave her safe home. The place she'd come to love. I would have loved Jasper even if I was still sleeping downstairs and working three jobs to pay for Heidi's care, but his desire to take care of her made me love him even more.

I would be the best assistant in the world. I'd make it up to him, if that were even possible. If something happened between us, I would find a way to pay him back. I wasn't going to tell him that now, but I would if that time came.

Believing in fairy tales wasn't smart. I'd never lived one and trusting anyone was hard. It wasn't smart, but he made me want to believe.

I stood in the yellow bedroom, looking at my limited wardrobe that didn't even take up a tenth of the closet space. I could put a bed in that closet and still have room. Heidi would think that was the coolest thing she'd ever seen.

I could visit her more now. Both Saturday and Sunday. Yet another thing to love Jasper for. He'd gone to the office and told me to stay home to move my things where I wanted them. Tomorrow I'd start the new job. I had tried to argue until he said please. So, I agreed and stayed home. Now that I'd moved everything, I felt lost with nothing left to do.

We needed groceries. I would do that and dust. Then I could make dinner. That should keep me busy. Heading downstairs, I heard voices and I paused. I was supposed to be the only person here. Had Portia returned? I listened carefully as I made my way down the stairs. It was a guy and a girl. No, it was two guys.

"I'll call Jasper and find out what the code to the pool house is," one of the guys said. I relaxed a little realizing it was just Jasper's friends.

I followed the voices and found them in the sunroom. I recognized Sterling and Tate. However, the girl I'd never seen. She was tall, slender, and gorgeous. Long, dark, almost black hair hung in loose curls down her back. Her high cheekbones and perfect nose gave her the look of wealth.

"There she is," Sterling said smiling at me. "I was about to call Jasper. The pool house is locked and we are starving. Could you tell me the code and fix us lunch?" His smile was friendly.

"Yes, of course. 49287 is the code," I told him.

"I want to lay out. Bring the lunch outside please. And I'd like a martini," the girl said as she stared at me the same way Stone did. Except she seemed more annoyed with my presence than he did.

"Okay," I said. "Can I get either of you a drink too?" I asked.

"Bourbon," Tate said, then winked.

"Whatever good beer Jasper has," Sterling replied.

"I'll have those out shortly," I told them and went to make their drinks. I wouldn't be going to the grocery today after all. From the looks of the woman I'd be busy. She reminded me of Portia. She was going to be hard to please, and would keep me hopping.

I made the drinks, then delivered them. Just before I walked inside I heard Tate call the woman's name. "Maisie."

I paused and my stomach knotted up. That was the girl Jasper had broken up with before he returned here. Why was she here now? Had he known she was coming? If he did, why didn't he tell me?

This was what I had been scared of. His world and mine. We didn't fit. I wasn't anything like her, and I never would be. I tried not to think of our drastic differences as I made a strawberry avocado salad to serve them while I made pasta for their main meal. No matter how hard I tried to push my worries away, the more they plagued me.

Each time I took something out to them, she found something else for me to do. She needed a towel that was plusher than the ones in the pool house. She wanted her martini dirtier. She needed tanning oil. Then that was the wrong kind. She needed one with less SPF. She wanted a sparkling water. She hated avocados. She wanted a spinach salad with pine nuts and strawberries. She was driving me crazy.

The more she asked for—or rather demanded—the less time I had to think about why she was here. The day went by quickly. When I was headed outside with her third martini order, I saw Jasper before I heard him. Taking a deep breath and reminding myself to smile. I went outside.

"The hard to get thing isn't attractive, Jasper. You wanted space. We had space. Don't be ridiculous," Maisie said sounding amused with him.

"There's Beulah," Sterling said with a bright grin. "Bring Jasper a drink. He needs one."

Jasper turned then to see me carrying a tray with Maisie's martini on it. He looked at the drink, then at me. "Have you been doing that all day?"

I glanced around to see all their eyes on me. "Yes." I wanted to crawl to my basement room about now. This was something I hadn't thought about. Facing his friends about us.

"Fuck," he said walking over to take the tray from me. "She's not your goddamn servant. He tossed the tray and the drink went flying, glass shattering everywhere.

"Jesus, Jasper! What is the deal?" Tate asked, climbing out of the pool, his eyes wide.

"My deal is you come into my house. Bring her," he said pointing at Maisie, "and don't think to fucking ask me. That's the deal. And you boss my girlfriend around like she's your slave. And because Beulah is the sweetest person I know she takes it." He looked back at me. "Did you feed them?"

I nodded, almost nervous to say yes. He winced. "God. I'm so sorry," he said to me before turning back to them.

"Did you call the help your girlfriend?" Maisie asked, her tone had gone from amused to angry. She was sitting up straight now from her lounged position. There was fire in her eyes.

"Holy shit," Tate said in a whisper loud enough for us all to hear him.

"Wow. Wasn't expecting that," Sterling added.

"You need to leave. Pack your shit and get the hell out of here. We broke up, Maisie. Do you not remember that? I thought it was very clear. You coming into my home uninvited and acting like you own the place is typical of you. One of the many reasons I'd never want to try that again. Go."

He turned around and walked toward me. His arm went around my shoulders. "I'm so fucking sorry," he said as he walked us back inside the house.

"You threw the drink." That was all I could think to say.

He chuckled. "Yeah. I might have lost my shit for a minute."

"I didn't mind serving them."

He shook his head. "You might not have, but I did. She shouldn't be here. You live here, you do not work here. I wish you'd called me. "

"I thought you knew."

"If anyone ever comes in this house and I haven't spoken to you about it, I don't know. I've not had time to talk to anyone. No one knows about us yet. But they will now. Which is good. They all need to know."

"She's beautiful, but she's not nice." I told him.

"She was in the beginning. I had been searching, hoping she was different. She wasn't. She was a fantastic actress."

I could see that.

"I'll deal with them. You don't have to see them again. If you want, just head upstairs. Take a bath, relax."

Other than Maisie, these were his friends. If I had any hope of fitting into his world I had to fit in with his friends. Running from them wasn't fitting in. "I'd like to stay. They're your friends. I need to get to know them."

He studied me a moment. He looked unsure. Concerned. I couldn't have him protecting me all the time. He'd get tired of that. Finally, "Okay. Let me make sure Maisie is gone. Then you can come out and join us. I won't run them all off. Just her."

"Thank you."

His frown increased. "Why are you thanking me?"

"For allowing me to find my place in your world."

He chuckled then. It was soft and the look in his eyes said so much. "You are my world, Beulah."

I didn't have any words that seemed adequate to respond to that. Instead, I managed a nod and a smile. One I felt deep inside.

"Let me go out there and deal with Maisie. Then I'll come get you. Sterling and Tate can get to know you as my girlfriend. Not the help."

"Okay," I agreed. I started to clean the kitchen from earlier when I had cooked dinner.

"Don't do that," Jasper said walking up and wrapping his arms around me.

"Why?"

"Because you aren't the help."

I leaned back into him. "If we were normal. If you were a regular guy and this was your apartment, would you argue with me about cleaning up after entertaining your friends?"

He was quiet as he held me. I gave him time to think it through. He'd never been a regular guy. It was something I wondered if he could comprehend. Did he know how normal people lived at all? Had he ever been around it?

"I think I understand what you're saying. If this makes you feel good, then do it. I won't dictate what you do. I just don't want you to do things because you think you're supposed to."

I nodded. Because I understood. Even if deep down he didn't.

Chapter Thirty

JASPER

TATE AND MAISIE were both gone when I stepped back outside. Sterling remained. He was sitting on the lounger with a beer in his hands and lifted his head to meet my gaze when I returned.

"Tate helped her take her things to her car. She drove. We'll need a ride when we leave."

I didn't care what they needed if that meant she was gone. I just needed her to be gone.

"We thought you'd be happy she wanted to get back together. Didn't know. Sorry."

I nodded. I hadn't told them or anyone about my catching her coming onto Stone. I'd let them all believe she ended things with me. My funk had been about returning here. Facing my life, the one I had no choice in. The one that was always empty. The void I had countless parties to try and fill. They had all assumed I was in a mood over Maisie. They knew now.

"So, the help," Sterling said with his eyebrow raised.

"Don't call her that. She has a name. Beulah. And she's not the help any longer. Although you all treated her like it today."

"Sorry about that too. In our defense, last time we were here she was, in fact, the help. Why didn't she correct us? She just let us order her around."

Because she was Beulah. She was kind. She didn't have an ego. "She's the most genuine person I've ever known. She didn't wait on your asses because she thought she had to. She did it because you're my friends, and this is my home. She was making sure you felt welcome."

Sterling frowned. "Really? That's . . . different."

"That's Beulah," I replied.

"Damn, man. When you change shit up, why don't you let us know? That was completely unexpected," Tate said as he walked back through the entrance gate.

"I was unaware you would be coming unannounced for a visit."

"We always come unannounced," Tate reminded me. He was right. I'd never had an issue in the past. I wanted them here. Anyone to help me deal with this place. With my mother.

"I know. And it's fine. I should have told you but things changed fast. There wasn't time to tell anyone."

"Can't say I blame you. I've thought she was smoking since the first day I saw her. Couldn't figure out how she'd managed to get Portia to hire her," Sterling grinned as he took a drink of his beer.

They didn't get it. I could try and explain that she was more than just gorgeous. But I knew them well. They wouldn't understand. They hadn't had a Beulah walk into their lives. They'd lived similar lives to my own and it was foreign to them.

"I'm going to get Beulah. You can start over, and apologize for ordering her around all day. Not for her sake because she doesn't expect it. But it'll make me feel better. Not much. But some."

Tate looked back at the pool house. "So we fix our own drinks, right?"

I wasn't even going to respond to that.

"Jesus, dumbass. Yes," Sterling replied with a shake of his head.

"Just checking. Is the bar in there stocked?"

I turned to get Beulah. Tate could fend for himself. I had no idea if the pool house bar was stocked or not. But he had two fucking legs. He could see for himself.

Beulah was wiping down the bar in the kitchen when I went in to find her.

"You can't stop cleaning, can you?" I asked amused.

She shrugged. "I clean when I get nervous. I can't be still."

I walked over and took the rag from her hand, then pulled her into my arms. "There is no reason for you to be nervous. I got rid of Maisie. The two idiots now know the score. Let's go outside and try to enjoy their company. I'd like you to get to know my friends."

She nodded her head, then kissed my chin which was as high as she could reach. "Thank you."

Why she was thanking me after she'd waited on those three all day I had no idea. "You never have a reason to thank me. Now, let's go before I decide kissing you is a better idea and we end up in my room the rest of the evening."

Beulah laughed and nodded her head. Happiness was back in her eyes and the nerves she said she'd dealt with were gone.

I held her hand and walked her back through the house, then outside with the others. Sterling looked up at us immediately, but

Tate was on the phone with a beer in his hand now.

Sterling smiled at her. "Sorry about today. I had no idea. And the Maisie thing was bad. We should have called."

"Have you ever called before you came?" Beulah asked him.

"Well, no."

"Then why would you have started now? I didn't mind."

Sterling's eyes softened and I could tell he was sinking into it. She had that effect on people, although she didn't realize it. I would have to get used to seeing men look at her that way. A lifetime of it. I could handle it. I knew I was lucky. I also knew I'd never let her go.

"How exactly did Jasper convince you to give him a chance? The ugly bastard that he is?" Sterling was teasing.

She shrugged. "Oh, you know, promised me millions, a new car. I prefer a Mercedes. Maybe a little red convertible one. And then he said he'd get me a private jet so I could go shopping in Paris when my wardrobe needed sprucing up."

Sterling looked confused for only a second, then he burst into laughter. I was grinning like a fool myself. "Damn, she's awesome!"

I nodded in agreement then kissed her temple. "I told you the jet was for our six-month anniversary."

She sighed dramatically. "Dang. I was hoping it would be sooner."

"What am I missing?" Tate asked walking back over to us.

"How witty Beulah is. Stick around and you'll be trying to figure out how to steal her from Jasper like I am."

"There's always the jet," Beulah told him which made him laugh again.

Beulah and I were going to be fine. She was a charmer. It didn't matter the crowd, she could charm anyone just by being herself.

"We'll get that damn jet tomorrow," I said.

Beulah beamed up at me. "Or you could just order a really good pizza with everything on it. That or tacos. I love tacos."

"Please tell me we are keeping her," Sterling piped up.

"Oh, I am," I assured him, but I didn't look away from her gaze. This was all I wanted in life.

I'd order pizza and tacos. Fuck, I may even get a jet.

Chapter Thirty-One

BEULAH

A GENTLE TOUCH on my head caused me to stir. I opened my eyes after I felt a hand run through my hair. My head was in Jasper's lap. The only light in the room was the candle's we had lit after eating pizza and tacos with Sterling and Tate. Then Tate had found a movie he wanted to watch and we all settled in to watch it, but apparently, I'd leaned against Jasper's shoulder and fallen asleep. At some point, he'd moved me to his lap. Or maybe I had moved down here myself.

I turned until I was on my back looking up at him. "Hey," I said.

He smiled down at me. "Hey."

The movie was over, and the others were gone. I wasn't sure how late it was or how long he'd been sitting there letting me sleep on him.

"Sorry I fell asleep," I said, then had to cover my mouth as I yawned.

He smirked. "Yeah, it was hard having someone like you lay on me for hours. A real chore."

"It was rude of me."

"Completely," he agreed, then ran the tip of his finger down my cheek. "I can't believe you'd do such a thing." The amused gleam in his eyes made me smile. He liked teasing me and I enjoyed it.

The silence in the house and the candlelight made this perfect. We were here alone, looking at each other, and it was safe. It felt right. Had anything in my life ever felt this right? I wasn't sure. I couldn't remember if it did.

"Having to smell you and feel your soft body pressed against me wasn't that easy. It was incredible. I've never enjoyed watching a movie that much before. I wanted them to leave so I could pull you into my lap and wake you up with my mouth."

I was awake now. I shivered, excited at the thought.

"They're gone now . . . and I'm already awake."

His expression grew serious. Those eyes I loved to look into became dark. My body tingled with anticipation.

"You're so fucking beautiful," he said. His voice was low, his words were a gruff whisper. "They wanted to be me tonight. But who wouldn't? I saw them watching us. Looking at you. Wishing. They wanted what I had. I didn't like them even looking at you. It was insane. But I was jealous they got to see you like this. It was mine to see. You make me crazy, Beulah. I've never been crazy."

I sat up, and he took me by the waist and moved me to his lap.

"Straddle me." His words were a gentle command.

I did, but I didn't sit down. When I did, I'd feel his hardness were my throb had begun already.

"I don't want to share you with anyone. That's impossible, I know, but there's this dark need in me to have you all to myself. Seeing them look at you the way they did bothered me."

I ran a hand through his hair. "They'd just never seen a girl eat pizza and tacos before," I teased.

He chuckled. "Valid point."

Then he put his hands on my hips and pushed my hips down. The moment I pressed against his erection, pleasure shot through me. I moaned and it took all my willpower not to rock against him.

I leaned into him until our lips met, and instantly his hands were in my hair as he kissed me. Our mouths locked and the taste of him drew me in, closer. The darkness, flickering light, and being completely alone made it feel as if there was no one else on earth. Just us. Just this place where we could stay wrapped up in each other.

My heart pounded inside my chest so hard I was sure he could hear it. As his hands slipped under my shirt, he wrapped it in his fists and pulled it over my head. He broke our kiss only to dispose of the shirt. He wasted no time capturing my mouth again. I held onto his shoulders as he made quick work of my bra and then pulled it off my body. When he broke the kiss this time it was to lean back and stare at me. His hands were on my ribs. His thumbs barely caressing my stomach now bared to him.

I was breathing so hard my breasts moved in front of him, and his eyes heated as he watched. Both nipples ached for him to do something. I was ready to beg when he brought his mouth to the first nipple and pulled it in with his teeth, barely scrapping the tender area.

"Ah!" I breathed out the word, and my hands went to his head. I wanted to hold him there. To keep doing whatever he was doing with his mouth. I could feel it all the way to the area I was now pressing harder against his lap.

His mouth moved from one breast, leaving it with a kissing, then he took the other. I watched in fascination. I couldn't keep from making noises. Especially, when he bit down on my nipple lightly. Just enough to heighten the sensation.

When he finally looked back up at me, I was barely able to sit still. My body was craving more. "Lie down," he told me.

I was at his mercy. I'd do whatever he said at this point, if he didn't stop what he was doing.

I reclined on the couch, and as soon as my back hit the cushions, he was over me taking off his shirt. His shorts followed. All that remained on his perfect body were his black boxer briefs. I'd often wondered what he looked like in them when I did the laundry. Now I knew and my imagination hadn't done him justice. Not by a long shot.

He bent and pulled off my shorts. Then he paused, and his gaze met mine. He held my gaze while his fingers grasped my panties and he slowly pulled them down, baring me completely to him.

I'd never been naked like this in front of a guy. When I'd lost my virginity, I'd still had on my dress. It had just been pushed up. I thought being this vulnerable would scare me. But it didn't. I wanted this. Him.

His eyes trailed down my body. The heat from his eyes made me feel hot and flushed. Then he kneeled between my legs moving them apart. I didn't realize what was happening until he rested one of my legs over his shoulder.

I started to protest but his kiss on my inner thigh felt so darkly beautiful I couldn't say anything. He flicked at my skin with his tongue, and then his mouth was there. Where I had never been kissed before. The first swipe of his tongue sent a sensation through me, causing me to cry out as my head pressed into the sofa cushions under me.

"God, you taste as good as you smell," he said lifting his head barely to look at me. Then he watched me as his tongue came out and he licked me again. This seemed forbidden, and although I knew people did it, I never imagined I would. It was incredible and lifted any barriers I had. Any that may have remained were gone as I trusted him to be intimate with me in such an erotic way.

My thoughts scattered when he pulled my clit into his mouth and sucked. I clawed at his shoulders. I cried out his name. I pleaded with him. I no longer cared about how I acted or looked. I just needed more.

He inhaled me as if I were delicious, and that made me even crazier.

When the wave washed over me taking me to my release, I began to shake and my thighs pressed against his head. I didn't want to come down from this high. I wasn't sure I could look at him after I had lost all control.

None of that was an issue because by the time I caught my breath, his body covered mine and I felt him pressing into me. "I can't slow down. Not after that. I've never been this fucking excited in my life," his voice was tense.

I couldn't speak yet. But I lifted my hips and opened my knees wider so he would sink inside me. He was larger than I was prepared for and the tight pain from his entrance while I was still coming off my orgasm brought me almost immediately back to climax—as if it was still happening.

"Fuck," he said against my neck. "Fuck, that feels amazing." He was breathing hard now. His body moving over mine as he began to move harder, faster. I was exploding again lost in my own world of ecstasy.

When he jerked his hips back and left my body, I started to reach for him. I wanted more. I wanted to go there over and over. But his own release shot all over my stomach as he let out a loud groan similar to a roar.

"Gaaah!" His hand worked as he pumped his seed onto me, panting as he watched it cover my skin.

"Shit, that was . . . I've never been that worked up," he said lifting his eyes from my stomach to meet mine.

I had no energy left. I was weak. But I smiled.

"I made a mess," he said once he could take a steady breath.

"I enjoyed making the mess," I managed to say.

He laughed softly then leaned over to grab his discarded shirt to clean me up.

When he was finished, he pulled me into his arms. I cuddled against him. His skin was warm and felt wonderful.

"I love you forever," he said.

And I believed him.

Chapter Thirty-Two
JASPER

I'D SENT BEULAH to spend some time with Heidi before coming into work. I wanted to make sure she saw her several times a week. Not just on Sunday's. The one thing I could get Beulah to do for herself was see her sister. When I told her to visit, she didn't argue. She went with a smile on her face that made the entire world seem brighter.

In life, I hadn't been taught to trust. It started with my parents. They lost my trust at an early age. Then there were friends, and eventually girls.

The only friend I trusted without question had been Stone. Simply because he was honest, even if it hurt. He didn't hold back punches. Neither had his father. Figuratively and literally. It was part of the reason Stone was so dark and hard to get close to.

Beulah was the first female I had ever trusted. She made it so damn easy to trust her. Watching her walk away, I never wondered if it was her sister she was going to see. I knew without a doubt that was where she'd be. It was a relief, knowing I could trust someone. Like a heavy burden had been taken away. Just another reason to make me love her more.

Coming home had sounded like living in the pits of hell. But I'd done it to see if I could even take the place my father had left for me. It had been time to try. He had left me more work than he knew. I came back for him, for the corporation he'd left me, and I'd found her. I would be forever thankful I did.

The door to my office opened without a knock. I knew before Stone stepped inside who it was. He was the only one who did that—came in unannounced. Even the woman I loved more than life would knock. I couldn't get her not to. She was determined it was the polite thing to do. Which made me smile more.

Stone would never be someone she liked or understood. I was okay with that.

He was wearing a white button down today which was rare. He still wore jeans though. He hated dressing like his father—the shoes he'd fill one day. If my father had beaten me until I was old enough to stop him, I'd feel the same.

"It's official then. You're in a relationship with her."

I nodded. "Yes. You knew it was headed that direction."

He looked annoyed. "I thought you'd be smarter. But it's your life. I can't live it."

"No, you can't."

He walked over and sat down on one of the leather chairs across from my desk. "Got any coffee?"

"I can have some sent up."

"Where's your secretary?"

"She's visiting her sister for a few hours because I thought it would be good for her."

Stone looked like he winced. "I should have seen that coming too."

I walked over to the phone and called Brandy Jo to have coffee sent up for the two of us. Then I turned my attention back to Stone. "How were things in Manhattan? As thrilling as ever?" I was being sarcastic. He hated it there.

He sighed. "Yeah. We managed not to kill each other. That's always a positive."

He was talking about his father of course. They were both tall, well-built men. His dad worked out regularly, and his newest wife was only three years older than Stone. The wife before her had been thirty. He was choosing them younger and younger the older he got.

"Assuming you know about me and Beulah from either Sterling or Tate, I guess you also know that Maisie showed up at the house."

He sneered as if her name disgusted him. "Yes, I know. And it was Sterling who called me. He's coming into the city next week and wanted to have drinks at Rauls one night."

A knock at the door stopped the conversation. "Come in," I called out.

Brandy Jo stepped inside carrying two coffee mugs and a smile that was never going to go away. I shouldn't have slept with her. She always looked at me like she was ready for round two. Even after I'd made it clear it was a one-time thing.

"Here you go gentleman. Can I get you anything else?" The tone of her voice had Stone rolling his eyes.

"No, that will be all. Thank you."

She ran her fingers over my hand as I took the cup. I quickly moved it away and turned my attention back to Stone. "Are you going to Spain next month?" I asked him.

He looked at her with his normal scowl, and she got the message that her flirting wasn't appreciated and left. "No. I don't think I am. Too much shit I have to handle. Moving into the flat in Manhattan from our house in New England is going to take some time. When are you going to pack your shit up and move it home?"

We'd shared a three-story house three miles from campus since our freshman year at Cuthdart. None of us had moved a thing. Tate was still living there when he wasn't traveling. He had one year left since he traveled for a year in Europe our freshman year.

"When there is time for me to leave here. I was going to hire someone to pack it up though. I don't want to leave . . ."

"Her," he finished.

"Yes, I don't want to be away from Beulah."

He drank his coffee and didn't say more about that. Which I could take as a step in the right direction. He was accepting our relationship, finally. I knew he would. He was just stubborn as hell.

"She's different. If you'd give her a chance you'd like her. You'd see why I love her. She's not a mistake. She's perfect. I can trust her. That's rare and you know it."

I expected a snide remark. Something very Stone-like. Instead, he stared out the window behind my desk a moment. Pensive. I let him think it through. At least he wasn't arguing with me. He'd let that go.

"I don't doubt what you are saying. I just don't think your world and hers will ever completely meld. That's all. You are in the honeymoon phase of the relationship. But when shit slowly starts to unpack itself from the baggage you both have, it won't be so damn pretty or easy," he paused then looked at me. "And are you sure you won't be the one to hurt her?"

It was rare that Stone pissed me off. Normally, I took his know-it-all attitude with a laugh. But this . . . He'd gone too far. I sat my coffee down and glared at him. Not looking away. Not giving him a pass because he was my best friend. "Are you questioning my love for her?"

He didn't back down. "Yes."

We sat there in silence, neither of us speaking. I was furious, but there were too many words to explain exactly how wrong he was, and I was calming myself before I started yelling.

The knock on the door stopped me, and as it opened, Beulah walked in.

Chapter Thirty-Three

BEULAH

STONE WAS BACK. My gaze went from Jasper to Stone, then back to Jasper. Maybe I should have waited until he said to come in. I didn't walk in any further. "I'm sorry. I can work somewhere else. I didn't mean to interrupt."

Jasper stood up from where he was perched on the edge of his desk facing Stone. They both looked serious but his face immediately softened as he walked toward me.

"You can walk in whenever you want. I've told you that," he said.

Yes, he had, but I also knew Stone didn't like me. "Okay," was all I said in return. Stone made me nervous. His presence just brought tension. I couldn't figure out why Jasper liked him so much. Sterling and Tate were much easier and enjoyable to be around.

"We were talking business and we're finished. Stone was leaving."

Stone didn't move from the chair. I didn't think he planned on leaving. I didn't mention it or look directly at him.

"I need to get to the filing. I'll be out of the way. Y'all can keep talking business."

"How was your visit?" Jasper asked.

"Great. Heidi was so excited to see me. She wasn't expecting me, so it was a treat. Thank you."

He cupped the back of my head and kissed me. It was deeper than I was comfortable with Stone in the room, but I kissed back.

"Don't thank me for that," he whispered against my lips then pressed one more kiss to my mouth before letting me go.

"Please continue to suck her face while I'm present. I don't mind at all," Stone said in his deep voice, sounding unamused.

Jasper rolled his eyes and gave me a crooked grin. "Ignore him."

That was hard to do. "I'll get to work," I said again, then hurried out of the room to the filing closet.

"Are you always going to be an ass around her?" I heard Jasper ask him.

"More than likely," he replied.

I closed the door between us and let out a relieved sigh to be away from him. I hoped Stone wasn't back to stay at the pool house. I didn't think we'd ever be okay together. He wasn't going to approve of this. Not the way the others had.

I'd had a wonderful morning with my sister, and I wasn't about to let Stone ruin my mood. I sat down and began working on the messy pile that I had barely made a dent in. The time ticked by, and it was lunch when the door opened and Jasper came walking inside.

"I'm starved. Come eat with me."

I stood up and straightened my skirt. "Sounds good. I'm getting hungry too."

He held out his arms and I walked into them. I liked this. Feeling like I had someone.

"Stone will thaw eventually," he said into my hair as he held me against him. "One day, the two of you will get along just fine."

I doubted that, but I hoped it was true. "If you say so."

Jasper laughed, then pulled back enough to kiss me. That was enough. Having him. His friends didn't have to like me. He did.

He held my hand as we made our way to the elevator. He wasn't hiding this. Whatever we were now he was making sure everyone knew. Brandy Jo would throw me out of a window if she got the chance. At least the pure hate in her eyes as we passed her in the lobby said as much. I would need to watch my back around her.

"Where are we going?" I asked and Jasper paused. His eyes fixed on something straight ahead. I followed his gaze and saw Portia stepping out of a black limo outside the entrance. This was going to mess things up. She would be even less thrilled about me than Stone.

I expected Jasper to let go of my hand, but his tightened around mine. I thought we were going to stand there like a wall to keep the evil out for a moment, but he began to walk moving us forward. It wasn't until the doorman opened the door and we stepped out into the sunshine that she saw us.

Her steps halted. Her eyes went from both our faces to our hands joined. I expected fury. Outrage. Or even a dramatic fit. But instead, there was fear. That, I didn't understand.

"I didn't think of this. I should have. She's gorgeous. Her gene's are excellent. You're a man and I left you alone with her. I just . . . I expected more of her. More determination. More pride."

Jasper was tense before, but his grasp on my hand was so tight now it was bordering on painful. I didn't say anything. "I won't allow you to hurt her or say anything to upset her. You'll be out without a dime. Do you understand me?" his tone was so cold it made me shiver.

Portia didn't look concerned. Her shoulders remained straight. Her head held in that lofty way I was accustomed to from her. "You've made a grave error, son. One that you'll no doubt blame on me, but one you were going to find out eventually. Secrets can't be hidden forever. I've learned that the hard way. But this secret? The lies? They have to come out now. It won't just hurt her, it'll hurt you both."

My heart began to beat nervously. There was something she hadn't shared. I knew there was a secret she was hiding. It was the only thing that made sense about her taking care of Heidi and me. I just couldn't figure out what it was.

"What the fuck are you rattling on about? I'm not going to waste time listening to your bullshit." Jasper looked unamused by Portia.

Her chin lifted and she sighed wearily. "I'll meet you both at the house in an hour. I have things you both need to see," she paused and looked from me back to her son. "So you can see I'm not rattling on about bullshit." Even when she cursed it sounded polished.

She turned on her heel, the chauffer opened the door of the limo, and she climbed back in. We didn't move until she drove away.

Jasper's body was wound so tight, he reminded me of a bomb about to explode. "We don't have to listen to her. Let's eat," his tone was hard and the anger was there sizzling.

"I want to hear what she has to say. This is about my mother. I know it is. I've always known there was something Portia hadn't told me. The reason she had helped us. After hearing all that, I think we should listen to what she has to say. I think we have to, Jasper. You hate her, but that doesn't make it okay to ignore this."

He took my hand and tugged me to him. Then he held me there tightly as if I were about to evaporate. Like I would leave him for good. "I don't trust her. She is going to try and end us."

I didn't think that was what she was doing. "Let's see her proof. That's all I'm asking. Hear her out."

He sighed and continued to hold me. We stayed that way for several moments. When he finally let me go he nodded once. "Okay."

Chapter Thirty-Four

JASPER

NOTHING HAD EVER terrified me like this . . . this unknown. Not even when my father had a heart attack. I
had never been so wracked with despair over possible impending
doom. I fought the urge to turn the car south and drive until we
were in the Florida Keys. Or west until we got to California. Or
even further away. Further from this. From my mother.

It wasn't her lies that scared me. I told Beulah it was, but it
wasn't. It was her secrets that I was afraid to face. She hadn't been
furious. She hadn't acted as if us holding hands was distasteful.
She'd been . . . different.

I didn't let go of Beulah's hand as we drove home. I needed
to feel her and to now she was there. That I hadn't lost her. This
wasn't over. It hadn't had a chance to really begin. We hadn't spent
a holiday together. We hadn't danced. We hadn't been on a date.

I wanted to take her to Paris, Italy, and Spain. Show her my
favorite places. Experience life with her. Maybe we should drive to

the airport now and fly away. Leave. Protect what we had. What we had found. Nothing my mother could tell me would change my love for Beulah. My need for her.

"I love you," she said softly.

"I love you," I repeated.

"This will be okay," she told me.

I wanted to think that too. But deep down the dread was there. I'd never been happy. She had been my first real glimpse at happiness, and I'd been stupid to think I'd keep that. I wasn't meant to have that in my life.

After I pulled into the drive, I parked the car and looked straight ahead. This was it. I had to trust what we would find out. Trust that Beulah loved me enough. That whatever horror my mother unveiled inside, we could withstand it.

"Let's go," I said, looking at her.

She nodded.

We walked into the house. Our hands no longer joined. The heaviness and ache of loss was already there. I couldn't fit the darkness that was already washing over me. It was going to be something that my mother had done. Something I was afraid Beulah couldn't forgive. A reason for her to run from here.

I stopped and grabbed her hand. "Don't hate me because of her. Whatever she's done, please love me. We will go far away from her. We don't ever have to see her again. Just . . . don't let her sins be mine."

Beulah smiled at me. Not her bright happy smile. A smile that was reassuring and she placed her hand on my face. "She can't make me stop loving you."

God, I hoped so.

We walked inside and found Portia in the great room. She

had a shoebox on the table and a glass with at least two shots of bourbon in it.

She turned to us and took a drink. "You both need to sit. A drink could also help."

We didn't take a drink or sit.

"Just tell us. Get this shit over with," I said, my anxiety still clawing at me.

She raised her eyebrows as if she didn't appreciate my speaking to her that way, then reached down into the box and took out a folded piece of paper. I watched her as she walked over to me and handed it to me. I stared at it as she held it out for me to take.

"Look at it. Then I'll explain."

Reluctantly, I took the paper and unfolded a birth certificate.

Reading, my first question was why did my mother have Heidi's birth certificate? But the sickness that grabbed me after I read Portia Edwards name as the mother almost knocked me to my knees.

I shook my head and moved away from her. "No. This, this isn't real." My world was spinning. So many questions I didn't want answers to. This was worse. Worse than my fears earlier.

"I was young and engaged to your father. I'd lived in a small two-bedroom home that didn't even have central heating and air. My parents were strict, religious people, and I hated the world I'd grown up in. Luckily, I had beauty. I used my beauty to get away from it all. I was about to have my fairy tale. The life I wanted. When a man that I considered an uncle, a deacon in the church, someone that everyone admired, raped me. I had been sent to take him a meal from my mother. She said he'd been feeling sick and she wanted to do the Christian thing, and send over a meal. I wanted my sister to take it but she was sick as well. She had been throwing up that week. No one knew why. Not yet.

"I took the meal, he wasn't sick. He was drunk and a big man. He was over sixty years old, but he was tall and kept in shape. He said things to me. Tried to get me to have sex with him willingly. I tried to fight him, to leave, but in the end, he won. I told no one."

"Two days later, my sister found out that her sickness was morning sickness. She was pregnant by the best-looking guy in town. He rode a motorcycle, lived for the moment, but he was going nowhere in life. My sister had fallen in love with him. He left town the moment she told him. My parents were going to send her away to have the baby then force her to give it up for adoption. Two days later, my sister was gone, leaving only a note apologizing. It was a scandal. One I hated her for." Portia stopped for a moment, thinking.

"Our family was now the talk of the town and I was sure I'd lose my fairy tale. I didn't though. He still wanted me. He didn't care about my sister or my religious, insane parents. We were engaged, and it wasn't until I was gaining weight I shouldn't have been that I realized I was pregnant. I thought it was ours. We'd been having sex for a while. We rushed the wedding and didn't tell anyone about the pregnancy. We went to Paris instead. I finished my pregnancy there. Away from his friends and our world. We'd return home after some time had passed, and take our baby with us. But she . . . wasn't okay. She had Trisomy 21, also known as Down syndrome."

"No!" Beulah's loud outcry sliced through me. She was backing away shaking her head. "That's . . . No!" she pointed at the birth certificate in my hand. "That is not Heidi. No. That is not Heidi's."

My mother looked at her then. Pity was in her eyes. She was

destroying Beulah and that was all she felt. Pity.

"We couldn't keep a child like that. I was young. We had society and this life to live. Travel, and well . . . she would be impossible. We discussed putting her in a home. But I couldn't. She was a baby. She needed a mother. So, I found the mother I knew would love her. Care for her. Take care of her. Treat her like she was her own. I found my sister."

Slowly, that one word took my heart and shattered it while disbelief and despair consumed me.

Sister.

"Pamela was my sister. She was younger than me. More beautiful than me, but she'd had eyes for the worst boy in town. She'd thought she could save him. She had been saving animals and nursing them our entire life. It was her way. I found her and her infant daughter in a trailer park living in poverty in Alabama. I gave her my daughter and two hundred thousand dollars. Then I walked away and never contacted her again. That was nineteen years ago."

This desperation was a nightmare that I'd wake up from any moment was all I could think right then.

"You left her. How could you leave her?" Beulah said in a whisper.

Portia took the remaining items from the box. A hospital bracelet, photos and a few letters. "Pamela still sent me letters with photos over the years. I never responded. But I kept them. You're welcome to read them."

Beulah stared down at the items in her hand, and I wanted to grab her and run. We should have gone to California. We should have left.

Beulah shook her head, and then backed away as if Portia

were dangerous.

"I can't. I can't be here." She shook her head again and started to leave.

"He's your first cousin. I didn't want to tell you, but y'all forced my hand by doing whatever it was you did. I'm not sorry for what I did. I'd have never been the mother Pam was. Never. Heidi had a better life with her."

Beulah stopped, and without looking back she replied. "I agree. She escaped life with a monster, and got to live with an angel instead. You're a horrible, horrible woman."

Then Beulah walked away.

I watched her go.

"You can't love her that way. It's incest. Disgusting."

I was too broken to respond.

I followed her, my entire body and mind numb knowing that the small joy I had was gone. Any hope I had was gone.

"Beulah," I called out and she paused. "We can run away."

She faced me then. Tears streaming down her face. "You can't run from this. It's ours to face," she let out a short sob. "Goodbye, Jasper."

My soul went with her as she turned and left.

ABBI GLINES

ABBI GLINES IS a #1 New York Times, USA Today, and Wall Street Journal bestselling author of the Rosemary Beach, Sea Breeze, Vincent Boys, Existence, and The Field Party Series . She never cooks unless baking during the Christmas holiday counts. She believes in ghosts and has a habit of asking people if their house is haunted before she goes in it. She drinks afternoon tea because she wants to be British but alas she was born in Alabama. When asked how many books she has written she has to stop and count on her fingers. When she's not locked away writing, she is reading, shopping (major shoe and purse addiction), sneaking off to the movies alone, and listening to the drama in her teenagers lives while making mental notes on the good stuff to use later. Don't judge.

You can connect with Abbi online in several different ways. She uses social media to procrastinate.

www.abbiglines.com
www.facebook.com/abbiglinesauthor
twitter.com/AbbiGlines
www.instagram.com/abbiglines
www.pinterest.com/abbiglines

books by
ABBI GLINES

As She Fades

ROSEMARY BEACH SERIES
Fallen Too Far
Never Too Far
Forever Too Far
Rush Too Far
Twisted Perfection
Simple Perfection
Take A Chance
One More Chance
You We're Mine
Kiro's Emily
When I'm Gone
When You're Back
The Best Goodbye
Up In Flames

SEA BREEZE SERIES
Breathe
Because of Low
While It Lasts
Just For Now
Sometimes It Lasts
Misbehaving
Bad For You
Hold On Tight
Until The End

SEA BREEZE MEETS ROSEMARY BEACH
Like A Memory
Because of Lila

THE FIELD PARTY SERIES
Until Friday Night
Under the Lights
After the Game

ONCE SHE DREAMED
Once She Dreamed (Part 1)
Once She Dreamed (Part 2)

THE VINCENT BOYS SERIES
The Vincent Boys
The Vincent Brothers

THE MASON DIXON SERIES
Boys South of the Mason Dixon
Brothers South of the Mason Dixon

THE SWEET SERIES
Sweet Little Thing
Sweet Little Lies
Sweet Little Memories

EXISTENCE TRILOGY
Existence (Book 1)
Predestined (Book 2)
Leif (Book 2.5)
Ceaseless (Book 3)

Made in the USA
San Bernardino, CA
15 February 2019